A hammock full of short stories

Written by

Jude St Clair

**Other books by
Jude St Clair**

2018 A cabin full of crime stories…

Published by
Jude St Clair

© 2017 Jude St Clair
Reprinted January 2018

Jude.StClair@hotmail.com
www.judestclair.weebly.com
Mandurah - Western Australia
ISBN: 978-0-6481952-0-7

Acknowledgements
The author would like to acknowledge her family and friends who assisted with reading, feedback and editing the many stories in this book. Special thanks to Olga and Gary Congdon (mum & dad) for all their help and encouragement.

Dedicated to my best friend, Shane.

Contents

The Keys

Keys glinting in the sunlight caught my eye. Picking them up I glanced around, looking for who might have dropped them, but in the busy, early evening crowd outside the station I could not spot anyone who fit the bill. Shrugging, I glanced at the keys again. There was a little blue key tag with letters on one side and a phone number on the other. Bringing out my mobile I dialled, waiting impatiently for someone to answer. Finally, a male voice, sounding exasperated said, "Yeah."

I quickly explained finding the keys after leaving the station and asked if anyone there might have lost them. The voice immediately softened and the man started thanking me, explaining how he must have dropped them when he left the train. Realising he didn't have them when he got to his car he'd arranged for a friend to come down with the spare set.

He told me he did not live far and he could pick them up now if that suited me. It didn't really as I was in a hurry to get home so I made a time for him to come to the apartment after dinner instead. We said our goodbyes, his suitably friendly now, I put the keys safely into my messenger bag and continued to the car.

On the drive home, my mind wandered to the voice on the other end of the phone. Although he sounded somewhat gruff to start out with, his voice turned friendly, with an unexpected, light, soft lilt to it. My active imagination ran wild, giving my mystery man a suave, dark and brooding look.

Ooo, probably an investment banker, a suit and tie type, driving a nice red convertible…I laughed, carried away with my daydream. It was a while since my last date and I hated to admit it but working in an all-girl office obviously affected me, I became very excited when talking to this man.

Arriving home to my little flat I quickly unlocked the doors, dropped my keys into the basket on the coffee table, and let out the new puppy. The little baby had been tucked away in the laundry for the day while I was at work. I kicked off my shoes, shook out my hair and slipped out of my work clothes. Oh, I do love these cooler evenings I thought to myself, and popped on a long, soft, thin jumper and some leggings, no shoes, no bra – now that's comfortable!

"Sorry, little Brooklyn," I murmured, "Only two more days then mummy will be home with you for a four-week holiday." Part of me felt sad that my new baby girl must stay home alone this week. However, considering she was a rescue pup the alternatives for her were limited. Her future looked bleak when she'd been found abandoned and undernourished by the side of the road leading to the rubbish tip. I spent the next hour playing, feeding, training and cuddling my little bundle of fluff.

After our cuddles I prepared myself a nice steak, a glass of red wine and a crisp salad. I added a drizzle of homemade balsamic dressing my mum brought back from her last trip down south.

Sitting to eat my dinner on the balcony - where I tended to eat all my meals when the weather permitted - I let my thoughts drift once again to the man on the phone. I pondered how tall he might be, and how old.

I conjured up a picture of a tall, sexy thirty-five-year-old with soft skin and olive complexion. At this point I started to feel a stirring in my loins that I had not felt for a long time.

I wonder if he has a girlfriend, or even a wife? Kids? Goodness, I never thought of that, he's probably a fifty-year-old family man with six kids at home, a golden retriever and a loving wife keeping house! I laughed out loud, startling poor Brooklyn, dozing with her head on my foot. Boy do I have an over-active imagination.

I did the dishes, cleaned the kitchen and was just about to pour another glass of wine when there was a knock at the door. Glancing at the clock I saw that it was a lot later than I thought. This could be the man for the key pick up. I straightened my hair as I scooted to get the door, not understanding why my heart was racing. I looked through the peephole and spied a tall, sandy haired fellow, clean-shaven with the bluest eyes ever. I called out, "Who is it?"

That lovely, lilting voice from the phone earlier came back with, "It's Tim, I've come to collect the keys?"

Opening the door, I smiled and said, "Oh hi Tim, come in, I was just being safety conscious." I giggled. Good grief, where did *that* come from?

As he brushed past me I felt a tingle where his arm lightly grazed mine and I could feel a blush creeping across my face. Unaccustomed to these feelings I managed to blurt out, "Just take a couch on the seat and I'll go get the keys."

We looked at each other and burst out laughing! "Well, that broke the ice," Tim said, grinning from ear to ear.

"I don't know about you but I was feeling a little tense. I don't get to visit pretty girls very often. I was quite thrown when you came to the door."

Blushing even further, I smiled, accepting the compliment and scooted off towards the kitchen to get his keys from my bag, picking up my glass of wine as I went.

"Lovely place you have here, looks like you're going for a Hamptons theme. I love the old-fashioned skirts and cornices."

"Th-Thanks," I stammered. Wow, not only is this guy drop-dead good looking but it seems he knows a bit about interior decorating and architecture too.

Tim continued, "I'm a chippie by trade but I specialise in high end carpentry. Specifically, period pieces and custom jobs. This is good work. And you've managed to incorporate an old-world charm in your shabby chic décor."

By this time, I was just about blown away, what more could a girl ask for? Piercing blue eyes, a body to die for, and he knew what 'shabby chic' was. Ha!

I realised then Tim was still talking, explaining how he must have dropped his keys outside the train station where he'd been meeting a new client. Feeling really frustrated at a fussy client he'd realised they were missing so looked about in the café and on the path but hadn't been able to find them. He then chatted away about how he was looking forward to the end of this week as he started his two-week annual leave this Friday.

Coming back into the room I asked, "Oh, so are you going anywhere for your holiday?"

"No, actually I am staying home to do some work around the house, laze on my new patio and take some well-earned down time. I also have a five-month-old dog that I can't leave alone. Rex is rather timid around people, he's a rescue through the local vet and I've been caring for him now for the past three months. He has come a long way since he first came home with me, but it's taking a lot of effort. He was abused I think."

Taking a seat in the lounge, Tim and I spent the next two hours chatting about rescue dogs, pets in general and the perils of puppies. I offered him a red wine and it was not until an hour or so later we realised there were one and a half empty bottles between us! I saw him glance at the clock then and finally handed over the keys I'd been fiddling with on the couch next to me all this time. He accepted them and stood up, looking a little nervous.

"Kirsty, I don't want you to think I'm being too forward or anything but I've really enjoyed this last couple of hours talking with you. I wonder if you want to get together for drinks or dinner or something Friday night?"

"That sounds great Tim, I have really enjoyed your company too. I would love to do dinner. You have my phone number, why don't you give me a call tomorrow and we can set it up."

Then Tim took his leave, I closed and locked the door behind him. All the while thinking how lucky it was I stumbled on those keys at the station. With a spring in my step I locked up, kissed Brooklyn goodnight and tucked myself into my warm bed.

As I gazed up at the ceiling, drifting off to dream of first dates, glasses of wine shared by an open fire, of snuggles and cuddles and movies together I was completely unaware of the eyes peering up through the darkness to my window. I did not see the smirk on his face as he twisted between his fingers the little container filled with putty he used to take a mould of my front door key. I was blissfully unaware of the ominous things to come…

Barking Dog

Gary slammed the phone down on the bench. That was the final straw. It was the thirteenth time he had called the council to complain about that damn barking dog next door and he'd been given the run around once again. Over the past few months they'd told him he would have to submit his complaint in writing, which he had done seven times now. Then they informed him the council rangers would look into it. He was told the rangers completed their enquiries and as no other complaints were received they would not be continuing to investigate. He'd even been told to just close his windows and turn up the tv by one cheeky council employee.

Well, Gary was fed up. He would just have to take matters into his own hands, as had been the case on several occasions in the last ten years. Being an animal lover, it tore him apart inside that these situations escalated, but he couldn't think of anything else to try. He'd started by having a friendly chat over the fence with the new neighbours when they first moved in back in April.

In May he jotted them a little note and dropped it into their letterbox one night, explaining that their poor dog missed them so much every day that he whined and barked continuously while they were gone.

Come June he'd stuck several post-it notes on their front door and made his first call to the council.

Now, here it was October and still that damn dog barked and barked every time his owners were at work or away from the house.

Why didn't they care? he wondered. How could they be so inconsiderate – not just of the dog, but also of the neighbours?

Gary strode through the kitchen, heading outside, nearly taking the flyscreen door off its hinges and stomped down the path to the potting shed.

"Ok," he mumbled, "I really have given them a fair go."

He gathered together his bits and pieces, placing ingredients into an old flowerpot, mixing them carefully together with a stick. Gary knew to wear gloves and a mask having been a landscape gardener for many years before retiring to this quiet, peaceful neighbourhood. He was highly conscious of the dangers of these types of chemicals.

After cleaning up Gary prepared his dinner and proceeded to indulge in his hobby of baking. It always seemed to have a calming effect on him. There was something therapeutic about creating beautifully shaped almond fingers, or a large tray of home-made chocolate chip cookies.

His dinner out of the way Gary took some of the special cookies, still warm from the oven and placed them in a Tupperware container lined with foil, taking care not to get any crumbs on his skin. He headed out to the yard to pay a visit to those troublesome neighbours and that damn dog.

Next morning when Gary awoke he felt unusually rested. He stretched and stood in front of his bedroom window. The street was lined with vehicles, including an ambulance, two police cars, and a ranger van.

He smiled to himself as he watched the council rangers loading the still barking dog into the van. He sincerely hoped its next owners would take better care of him, he really had a soft spot for dogs. He turned away as the two body bags were wheeled out to the coroner's van and went to pour his morning coffee.

Bus Stop

She gazes down the street, not really seeing the traffic, commuters hurrying past, parents taking children to school. Her eyes are trained to look for the bus. It's as if she has blinkers on, running her own, slow motion race. The bus the finish line. After all, she has waited here at this particular bus stop twice a week at this time for the past nine years.

The wet weather doesn't faze her. She's been here in rain, wind, bright sunshine - oh she does like those days when the sun is shining, it warms her hands, and with her arthritis that is a much-appreciated blessing.

But it's the times when it's snowing she loves the most. Arthur loved snow. For an eighty-two-year-old he certainly acted like a seven-year-old child when it came to snow! A smile fleetingly dances across her face, like a snow flurry, as she recalls the hundreds of snowmen she's helped him build over the years.

It's not going to snow today though, too much rain about. She doesn't even notice it seeping through her shoes, which have long since seen the day when they were waterproof. Her mind drifts to the flowers she carries. She tries tucking them into her basket, protecting them from the rain drops. They are a nice bunch today, baby's breath and carnations and, of course, the big orange gerbera in the centre…oh how Arthur loved his gerbera's… she jerks back to reality as the big green bus pulls up in front of her…

A Sunday Afternoon in the Boroughs of New York City

A true story. A snapshot of life seen through the author's eyes on her last visit to the Big Apple.

During the week this road in Queens is one of the busiest in the borough. Cars rush along here to take their passengers to work, shopping, appointments and more. Early this morning, at around 9am, there were cars everywhere, there were people dressed in their Sunday best, off to church. Families walking, couples holding hands. There is still a lot of traffic, but people are moving a little more leisurely now. I am sitting on a bench, in the shade, although currently it is a pleasant temperature outside. This is not your typical relaxation spot, at a six-road intersection. It's a paved area with seven or eight old maple trees, and a few young saplings, but it's a terrific people-watching point.

I while away the time, watching folk go about their business, relaxing, walking past for fitness, fun or fellowship. There is a market stall and a bake sale up the road. This is attracting a huge crowd of churchgoers. A constant stream of moms and bubs, dads and toddlers, grandparents and grandchildren parade past me. After several hours, just absorbing the atmosphere and admiring the humanity, I move on.

Brooklyn Ikea on a Sunday afternoon. The world and his mother have turned up for a 'day out'. The café staff are working overtime.

Pumping out cheap meals ($1.20 for a hearty soup, $2.15 for a huge bowl of 'help yourself' salad and 99c for a slab of princess cake – are you kidding me?) Most shoppers appear to be choosing the special - $3.99 for meatballs and unlimited fountain soda.

People are happy. The hum of conversation coming from the café has cheerful overtones, kids laugh, there are moms and dads with babies, a few young couples, a large group of twenty somethings and lots of girls with their sixty-year-old moms. There are extended families and multicultural couples everywhere.

Finally, I leave the store for the free shuttle bus to the station which leaves every fifteen minutes from directly out front. The bus is packed full, a woman with three kids, each one carrying a box or bag of goodies. Two pretty girls struggle, laughingly with a flat pack – it looks large enough to be a TV unit. A grandfather assists two young boys to get on the bus, all three have distinctive, bulging, blue Ikea bags, the recyclable ones, slung over their shoulders. We all pack ourselves into the bus, with our parcels, like giant jigsaw pieces, twisting and turning to make sure we get the best fit for our precious purchases.

Then we are off, the bus lurches forward, struggling under the weight of so many people with so much 'stuff'. Now we are wending our way through the back streets of Brooklyn to the subway stops.

We pass a huge oval that has four or five games of baseball happening. All ages. There is an adult game at one end, teens and even a 'little league'.

There are hundreds of spectators, literally hundreds, on the bleachers, on the grass, picnicking on lawn chairs.

Street vendors have pulled up their trucks, haphazardly, along the sidewalk and parked. Selling everything from good old-fashioned American pretzels to halal burgers and Spanish chorizo sausages. The ice cream van has a long line as the day has warmed up now to the high seventies. There are kids on scooters and teens on bikes and groups of girls giggling and preening themselves. We cross a major road and pull into a bus stop. Lo and behold, another oval with a park attached. This one has identical teams playing baseball, with spectators and families walking their dogs. The oval backs on to a massive tenement housing development. It overlaps with a large children's park, a skate arena and what appears to be eight back-to-back half courts of basketball. Six of these have either a team of young men playing or groups of four or six Afro-Americans standing around, shooting the breeze and shooting some hoops.

A couple of games look intense...shirts are off, dark sweaty bodies running around, occasionally crashing into each other, probably a bit more body contact than is truly allowed in the rules of the game, but everyone looks like they are enjoying themselves. I am sad when the bus pulls out into traffic and continues to the station. This looks like a beautiful place to be, on a Sunday afternoon in New York City. I make myself a promise to come back.

Iceberg

'Frigid.' That's what he'd called her. *'The Ice Queen.'* "Humph," she snorted.

When the two buckets were full Isabella took them out to the garage. She struggled a little as this was the sixth load and they were getting heavy. She was careful not to spill any and made her way gently around the pile of frozen food and tubs of ice cream and sorbet that were piled in the middle of the room. She opened the lid to the oversize chest freezer and emptied the contents of one bucket in.

She was in no mood for any more of his nonsense. All those years of tolerating his adulterous ways, turning the other cheek to his affairs.

Isabella poured the final bucket of water into the freezer, the liquid beginning to freeze almost immediately. It was cold this time of year in the forest where they lived in a little alpine house outside of Oslo.

She smiled sweetly down at Sven. The look of shock frozen on his face through the ice was amusing to her.

"Well honey, if I'm the 'Ice Queen', what does that make you?"

Mrs Isabella Bergen chuckled as she returned to the kitchen to make dinner.

"I guess you're now an ICEBERG-EN," she muttered.

The Nurse

She knew she shouldn't walk this way at night. Although when she'd parked here this morning the place had been bustling with cars, workers and tradesmen's vans. However, it was a different story now, at 11.45pm. The car park was nearly empty. The so-called security booth was locked up tight. More like a help desk for visitors who did not know where to park at the new hospital than any real provider of security. The guard usually went home around 8pm, when visiting hours were over.

Delores clutched her shoulder bag a little tighter and quickened her step. Damn, she thought, the light in the far aisle was out, right where her Toyota was the last car parked. This back corner looked like a giant black hole, with not even a glint of moon to shed some pale light. Hearing a rustling noise from the far garden bed caused her to turn sharply. Vaguely making out two little red eyes from under the bush on the left – she pondered, a possum or a rat? She fumbled in her bag for the keys.

The wind started to pick up, rustling papers across the bitumen. Delores would not normally have such a nervous disposition but there was something about a cold, dark night, being alone in a virtually empty carpark of a brand-new hospital. It was not even fully functional or completely staffed yet. There were entire wings still closed, dark and silent. It was no wonder she felt on edge.

Her ears were playing tricks on her now. She scrambled a little desperately for those keys. How hard can it be? It is not that big a bag, she admonished herself.

Finally, her fingers closed around the little cross that she used as a key ring.

Pulling out the keys, her hand shaking as once again, she turned to listen – was that footsteps she heard in the distance? She could barely put her key in the lock and willed herself the strength to turn it and unlock the door. Yanking it open, then collapsing inside, she threw her bag on to the passenger seat and quickly locked the door again behind her.

Letting out a huge sigh of relief she relaxed, taking a minute to get her breath back. I got myself a bit worked up there, she chastised herself as she smiled into the rear-view mirror. That silly, nervous smile of relief, that plays across your face when you have just got through a frightening experience.

"Breathe," she instructs, "Breathe Delores, breathe." She felt herself calming down as she took several long, deep breaths. "Ok, let's go now, nice and slow."

She reached out her hand for the keys but it seems that they had tumbled back into her handbag when she'd flopped into the car. As she grasps them, her fingers brush lightly against the hard, cold vial wrapped in a tissue and a wave of contentedness sweeps over her.

She remembered how, just a few hours ago, she was sitting and holding the old lady's hand as she passed into the next world to be with the Lord. How privileged she felt to be able to be there, comforting her in her hour of need. Delores silently made the sign of the cross and put the gold charm that hung under her nurse's uniform, to her lips.

To have been able to be a part of that beautiful woman's life these past two months, to calm her when she awoke from fitful sleep, to administer drugs to her when she needed them for her pain, to spoon feed her and see the gratefulness in her eyes.

She had become fond of the lovely Mrs Thomasina Sinclair. Delores enjoyed reading to her, a cheap paperback her son dropped off when people were around, but passages from the bible when she was on the ward by herself. Tomi, as she'd asked Delores to call her, so enjoyed Paul's letter to the Galatians and her favourite readings came from John's Gospel.

A tear edged its way out of her lashes and rolled lazily down Delores cheek. She delved into her handbag and dabbed a damp tissue to her eyes. It'd been difficult at first, this calling of hers. Taking a long time to come to terms with what she knew in her heart the Lord had planned for her. It wasn't as though she questioned his intentions or anything, but she wondered in the beginning if she had the internal fortitude and the strength of character to be able to get through the interrogations and the investigations.

The questions were always the same.

Q: Are you sure you gave her the correct dosage?
A: Of course! I am good at my job. I am a highly commended nurse, not some casual carer.
Q: Did you leave the bottle within reach?
A: Of course not. I've been attending terminal patients for over twenty years, I do not make mistakes.
Q: Could the patient have possibly reached out and taken the pills herself?
A: Well I hardly think so. She was incapable of lifting her head, let alone her arm and to reach a metre away to the table seems somewhat unrealistic don't you think? Besides, can't you tell how much of the prescription was in her blood at an autopsy?

Q: Was anyone else around at the time?

A: Not that I am aware of, but I was the only one on this ward so I don't have time to monitor the comings and goings of visitors that the receptionist lets through. That's her role.

This, being her nineteenth patient she had pretty much mastered it now. Delores smiled to herself, dabbed her eyes again and reached over to tuck the vial a little further down inside her bag. Long ago she had discovered that epinephrine was surprisingly easy to come by in her workplaces and didn't show up in a regular autopsy.

It was only discoverable if a test was specifically requested by the coroner, which of course would never be the case with these, terminally ill patients. She wiped her tired eyes with the wet tissue one more time and started the car. It was only a short trip out to the freeway, then in fifteen minutes she would be home. There was a well-earned two-day break coming up and she was looking forward to doing a bit of gardening.

Delores turned on to the ramp, leading to the freeway and shook her head back and forth, blinking her eyes as her vision appeared a little bleary. I am tired today, she admitted to herself, I need to cut back on a few shifts I think. Perhaps I'll look at just working part-time in the next hospital. Still, she could worry about that next month. She had one more patient to help here at this hospital first, before she would look at moving on to the little private hospital she'd researched in the city.

It was at that moment that everything went black. Within seconds Delores hands instinctively left the steering wheel and clutched at her chest. Her foot depressed the accelerator and the little blue Toyota bounced over the curb.

It shot along the guard rail before flipping four times and coming to rest upside down against the limestone retaining wall on a new housing estate.

The smell of burning rubber permeated the air and a fireball erupted with a bang, from under the bonnet.

The coroner ruled it accidental of course. A tired nurse on the way home from a long, traumatic shift. Coming to light that Delores had lost one of her terminally ill patients that day too.

They'd made the identification from dental records as there was not much left after the fireball. Certainly not a handbag on the front seat, containing a large, cracked vial of epinephrine, leaking into a tissue, and very clearly labelled.

WARNING:
HIGHLY TOXIC.   POISONOUS CHEMICAL.

Avoid all contact with skin, clothing and particularly the eyes. DO NOT ingest. If ingestion or skin contact occurs call a Physician or Poison Control Centre immediately.

What is a Drabble?

Drabble

*A **drabble** is a short work of fiction of exactly one hundred words in length, not including the title. The purpose of the **drabble** is brevity, testing the author's ability to express interesting and meaningful ideas in a confined space.*

Beautiful Music

Thank you for the music, the songs I'm singing…for all the joy they're bringing. Celebrating life events…

Nursery rhymes - kids learn their ABC's. Teens bonding over Metallica or Brittany.

Date night, listening to crooners like Deano, a million tears shed to Lorretta or Kenny.

'The Wedding March.' 'When a Child is Born.' 'Congratulations,' at a graduation.

The final funeral hymn – 'Amazing Grace,' or 'Abide with Me.'

But the music to my ears will always be – Dr. Graeme Clark – a cochlear ear implant, and my little girl saying, "I can hear Mummy – I can hear the music – and it's BEAUTIFUL!"

Lilies

On the ninth day of the month, when the noon bell rang, they gathered in the village square, not one, excepting Mikey, daring to be tardy. The air was heavy, the previous night's rain still threatening, the pavement glistening. Nevertheless, not even the wintery weather could dampen the spirits of these young lads. For this was the day they had all been dreaming of. The day all their hard work paid off. Today these twelve young boys would finally become men.

"Where's Mikey?" whispered Julian.

"No idea," said Robert, shrugging his shoulders, but looking a little worried.

Just at that moment Michael Johnson appeared. He darted around the corner of the village bakery and scooted across the edge of the square to join ranks with the others. They were all standing nervously, trying not to move in their freshly ironed khaki uniforms, buttons sparkling, creases knife-edged.

"You only just made it," Julian said quietly.

"It's all good," replied Mikey with his famous grin.

"Attention!" The command came from the Captain who took his position at the front of the square, right in front of the Post Office – well, it was more like a little room really, with a desk, a chair, and a cupboard. After all Rampart could only boast 412 official inhabitants, 413 if you counted the homeless fellow they called 'the Troll' who lived under the bridge, but no-one ever knew if he was around, he seemed to go missing for weeks at a time. So, the little Post Office, that also served as the Tax Office and the Army Recruitment Centre coped well.

Mikey, Julian and Robert stood tall and straight faced, except for a tiny grin Robert flashed to young Suzie Wilkinson who stood next to Robert's mum. She was dabbing at her eyes and beaming proudly at her new fiancée. The shiny ring on her finger was sparkling in the sunlight and Robert grinned just a little wider with pride.

"...to do us proud. God speed men," the Captain was just finishing his speech. The crowd all rose to their feet and started applauding and smiles graced the faces of the twelve nervous, yet excited young men.

"Dismissed," the Captain shouted and as one a cry of "Hoorah!" rung out over the square. Twelve shiny caps flew into the air and the men began receiving congratulations from their family and friends. Mikey stood slightly away from the crowd, alone. Not having any parents, or a girlfriend, he was not fully included in the celebrations, but that did not detract from the sense of pride he felt.

Slowly the crowd parted and the transport truck from the nearby air force base crawled onto the square. The Captain silently motioned for the boys to fall in, picking up their caps and their duffle bags and giving their loved ones a final salute they headed off to bravely represent their town and their country in a far-off land...

The sun was slowly setting when the old lady rose from reminiscing on the bench seat in the memorial garden. She took her basket of lilies and laid one on each of the twelve headstones. "Proud of you boys. I will never forget you," Suzie whispered, then hobbled off home to make supper for herself.

22

Pedicab Paul

He hated this part of it. Having to smile and pick up a couple of legitimate customers in the pedicab during the day. He knew it was essential for his success though. To continue his important charity work and to provide for his family he must be seen occasionally, at various times and on different days, riding around the seventy-eight main blocks of the French Quarter. Over the past couple of years, he'd learned not to pick up certain customers if he could possibly avoid it. The older American tourists were the worst. They wanted to take selfies with you, expected you to give a full running commentary while you rode and they always tried to get something more for their money, an extra five minutes, a block or two over what they'd agreed upon. Pigs! He'd discovered the best ones to pick up were the young, drunk couples. They usually just wanted a lift back to their hotel because they were way too wasted to walk, or were disorientated and lost their way.

Like most of them in New Orleans, Paul's pedicab was yellow. It was faded with some of the paint chipping off – exactly as he designed it. Half the registration number was unreadable and even the advertising panel was barely discernible. It could possibly have been a child smiling at a puppy, or some sort of animal and the words ALL AMERICAN and part of a local phone number. He'd printed it on himself, based on research he'd undertaken on the other local pedicabs.

They parked regularly outside Harrah's Casino and over near the Natchez paddle steamer so they were easy to watch.

Those few marketing units he took at night school many years ago paid off as he assessed and surveyed what people tended to remember from glimpses of advertising on cars, buses, cabs, trolley cars and other moving vehicles. The last thing he needed was for his pedicab to stand out from the others.

Paul smiled and nodded politely at the young woman who asked if he was available.

He tipped his cap to her, "Certainly Miss, where would you like to go today?" Paul went to help her get her obviously drunk or stoned partner into his vehicle. "I got you sir," he said to him, trying not to get too close so the smell of vomit didn't permeate his clothing.

"I'm a-a-alright. I can do it. Don't worry about me brother," the young man slurred belligerently, then proceeded to lean first on this girlfriend, then on Paul, before falling into the cab, right across the seat. The woman rushed around to the other side and straightened him up while smiling apologetically.

"Just to the Embassy Suites on Julia please," she replied as she settled herself in, removing her partner's groping hands and placing them on his own knees.

Paul took them to their destination quickly, without having to give any tourist chatter, accepted her $10 fare plus a $5 tip with a little bow and touched his cap again to say thank you.

The doorman rushed out to assist her with her young man. *Thank God for doormen,* he praised. *I certainly wasn't going to help get the big redneck inside.*

At that moment he decided to head home. Putting in a solid four hours, taking nine customers around, he'd managed to cover at least half of the quarter. More than enough activity to keep up the little charade so he started for home with renewed vigor. Paul was eager to get back to his family especially as he would have to be out working again tonight.

Whipping out his keys he then unlocked the old gate in the side wall of his condo. He'd put a lot of time and effort into choosing this new residence a couple of years ago when moving here from Binghamton in upstate New York. It needed to meet some stringent requirements for his special family. Most importantly the building needed to have a minimum of two exits. This one had three – the fire escape on the side of the building, the front door which led to the gate and the sidewalk and the wide, rusty old gate in the side wall of the courtyard.

The yard needed enough room to store his pedicab out of view of the street. He knew drivers who kept their bikes chained up to poles in the street outside their homes and the ones owned by the businesses were returned to their headquarters at the end of each shift but that wouldn't have worked for Paul. It was important his coming and going at all hours of the day or night not be the subject of scrutiny by nosy neighbors. It was also essential any tenants or owners living in the building were not too inquisitive and in that respect this condo in Burgundy street was perfect.

The downstairs apartment at the left of the building was used purely for storage by the café across the road. Staff from there would come over maybe once a week to get a replacement table, or a couple of boxes of napkins.

25

The two up-stairs condos were owned by a couple from San Francisco who'd bought them with the intention of doing a bit of renovation and renting them out, however they had split up and now those apartments were vacant, waiting for the court to decide who was the rightful owner. The fighting going on for three years according to Ritchie, the old vet Paul had befriended before deciding to buy the condo and move in. Ritchie Gordon lived in the building next door and was also a perfect neighbor. He kept himself to himself.

A bonus that there was no family or friends to come visit, however, he knew everyone and everything that went on in his part of the quarter. He was a valuable source of information and a gauge for Paul because if Ritchie didn't notice him coming and going late at night or early in the morning then no-one would.

Paul managed to purchase the right-hand, downstairs condo with its small front facing living room, generous rear kitchen, spacious separate bedroom and large bathroom. Best of all it had a basement.

He had also negotiated the use of the vacant two-story servants' quarters at the rear of the complex in return for maintaining the courtyard and breezeway – basically minor gardening, watering a few plants and sweeping once a week. He told the previous owners he would use the extra building for his 'hobby' which he described as organic preservation.

They presumed it was to do with preserving fruit, or flowers, which made him chuckle. Little did they know there was something much more sinister being 'preserved' behind the blacked-out windows.

After covering his cab with plastic - you can never tell what's going to happen with Louisiana weather, it can change three times in a day - he opened the back door to his apartment, singing out, "Hi family, I'm home!"

With a huge smile on his face he tossed his keys on the bench and headed straight to the front room. He loved to call it the 'parlor' because that sounded so classy. He often said to new guests or family members who came "Welcome to my parlor," and he'd use a British accent. They'd laugh and enter with enthusiasm. Mostly the laughter would only last a few seconds, until their brains caught up with what they saw in front of them, but he did enjoy those few moments.

"Hey guys. I missed you so much. It's lovely to be home with you all again."

Paul bent to kiss his 'Mom' on the top of her head and patted his two sisters' heads as he moved along the back of the couch. "Have y'all had a nice day? Shall I put the game on TV now?"

Paul moved past his 'pops' sitting slumped in the recliner near the window and he picked up the TV remote. He changed channels to the local sports network where the Saints game was due to be televised this evening and he lowered the volume.

"Oh my, you look like you have a touch of the sun honey," Paul turned to his 'girlfriend' and proceeded to pick her up from the chair facing the window.

He lovingly arranged her in a better position on the two-seater love chair and after moving his 'little brother' and his pet dog Fido out of the way he sat next to his girlfriend Julie and gently placed her hand in his.

He had long ago adapted to the shock of touching cold, dry skin, although he admitted it might be getting near to the time when he would have to go looking for a new girlfriend.

Paul especially enjoyed doing their hair, but sadly it did become a little bit unpleasant to touch after a couple of weeks. Often after dinner he would spend hours grooming his beautiful family and he would always spend extra time on their hair. He loved his family so much.

His dad in the recliner was about seventy he guessed. He'd picked him up near the bridge where the old man was slumped against a building, passed out drunk.

Dad cleaned up well though once Paul took him home. He had gently administered the anaesthetic, then set about the ritual of washing and grooming, putting on the new clothes, shaving and giving him an expensive hair treatment.

Being a family member for just over two weeks now he was still looking great. He'd taken over the position in the recliner from 'old dad' who'd only lasted with the family for four weeks.

Old dad, a transient from Denver, who through poor life choices or circumstances ended up down on his luck. Paul felt proud when he was able to provide him with such a comfortable, loved environment for his last month on this earth, probably better than anything the old fella ever experienced in his life before.

He had laid his dad to rest the day after 'new dad' came to live with them. Taking the old truck out of the storage unit where he kept it over in mid-city he gave his dad a final ride through the crescent city, along the river to the bayou, late on a Sunday evening.

Paul had explained to Dad it was time now, time to move on to another place, reassuring him he would always be remembered as lots of photos were taken for the family album. After he loaded Dad on to the flat-bottom boat he kept tied up in an overgrown part of the levee he paddled out to the camp his very first 'dad' left to him a few years ago and spent the night out there in the quiet with him. Paul considered it a stroke of luck, or good fortune his first dad hadn't any friends or relatives who knew about the camp, so Paul took it over and looked after it for him after he passed. Upon awaking early, the next morning he laid Dad gently to rest in the open cage he built especially for this purpose and lowered it into the water.

He called softly "Good-bye Daddy," then returned home, comforted in the knowledge that by the time he arrived home the 'gators would have disposed of the body completely and all the clothes would have been destroyed in the sealed furnace he had installed inside the camp a couple of years ago.

Paul broke his reverie and arose with a sigh. "Well, I would love to stay and watch the game with you guys but I have chores to do and dinner to prepare before going out tonight. You will all be pleased to hear I will have some exciting news for you when I get home."

He started his rounds then, tidying up, putting a load of washing on, vacuuming. He had discovered long ago that with his special needs family he needed to maintain his house meticulously. It was necessary to clean with strong disinfectants.

Obviously, he was meticulous with his family's ablutions, but having a large family like his, cooped up inside the apartment all day, there were bound to be some unpleasant odors at times. The lights came on as Paul prepared his evening meal.

Due to the nature of his night time charity work he had designed and installed a complex system of automatic lighting and power. The television would turn itself off at 11pm each evening, and on again at 8am. The parlor lamps and kitchen lights would turn on and off too. He'd removed the timers from the bedroom lamps though as there were some nights when he was home and wanted some intimacy with his girlfriend and it certainly wouldn't be appropriate for lights to turn on in the middle of that. The radio in the kitchen had a timer also, coming on at 10am, softly, and set to play a station of mostly talk back radio.

Paul was particularly proud of this idea as it would give the impression of people chatting in the kitchen if ever someone should come to the door, or god forbid, enter the courtyard.

One of his favorite sayings was 'Necessity is the mother of invention' which apparently was accredited to Plato. He totally believed this and had many 'inventions' to prove it.

After putting on a small piece of beef to simmer with some potatoes and carrots he decided he had time for a quick shower before he ate. "Hey Julie," he called, "Want to take a shower with me darling, before dinner?" "Well of course I do, you handsome man," Paul whispered to himself. He picked up the doll-like figure sitting on the couch and took her into his bedroom.

He had realised about six or seven girlfriends ago that his family required a lot more work to look after than a 'normal' family, but like any loving son, husband or father he was tireless in his efforts to do the best he could for them. Gently spreading out an old shower curtain on the twin bed on the far side of the room he carefully undressed Julie and then proceeded to give her a 'shower'. He sponged clean every inch of her body, drying and then moisturising her with a special lotion he developed last year.

Over time Paul overcame many challenges faced by his special family but he was particularly fond of the lotion he had developed for them and what he liked to call their 'skin conditions'. To maintain their deteriorating skin, he had turned to a range of solutions and it wasn't until he studied the art of taxidermy, and in particular the mounting of fish, that he experimented with injecting different kinds of salt (borax, potassium alum and ammonium alum).

He soon discovered the alums were made of molecules too dense to permeate the skin. However, with a cocktail of thinners, adhesives and the addition of his own invention of shellac he developed a lotion enabling the skin to retain its moisture, shape and texture to about 75% of the original for a couple of months after the host had been paralysed.

It had taken quite a few years for Paul to come to terms with the multitude of special needs his family demanded. He had learned to live with the constant, cold, 55° temperature he maintained in his apartment and accepted having to keep thick, heavy curtains over his windows.

At first the smells, dryness of the skin, brittle hair and glassy eyes would make him sad, angry, and in the beginning, even disgusted at times.

However, Paul regarded himself as a kind man, a man who cared about humanity and people as individuals. Never discriminating because of race, color, gender or sexual orientation. Treating all people the same and learning to accept and live with certain hardships so he could have a beautiful, ever changing family to take care of and love. He had his night time charity work, his family, but most days he wished he could do even more.

"There you go my darling," he whispered lovingly in Julie's ear. "All clean and I must say you look particularly gorgeous tonight in your black negligée." He carefully moved Julie to the queen bed in the centre of the room, turned on the TV and set her up to watch the quiz show Jeopardy, something they liked to watch together at dinner time.

After showering quickly and dressing in his usual all black night work clothes he dished up his dinner and brought it back to the bedroom to eat on the little fold up table he kept next to the bed. Just in time he thought, as the distinctive Jeopardy melody came on. The next hour whizzed past and Paul finished with eighteen correct answers, did his dishes and tidied the kitchen. He said farewell to all the family in the parlor and then tucked Julie under the covers in their bed, giving her a long cuddle before setting off in the pedicab for his charity work.

Tonight, he headed uptown, across the warehouse district, passing the bridge and the numerous homeless people who camped there.

Making good time and arriving at his destination, the Walmart on Tchoupitoulas by just after 9pm. This side of town was dark, with few working street lights but he knew exactly where he was going as he had spent five nights over the past two weeks doing his research. He knew there was a group of three women who had been camping out behind an abandoned warehouse two streets over. He had watched them come and go, plying their trade late into the night, earning a few dollars off the tourists on Canal Street, then wasting it on drugs and alcohol.

They were so dirty. It appeared they had been wearing the same clothes for two weeks. He didn't think they had washed them and doubted they had even washed themselves during that time. Paul was appalled. How disgusting, he cringed. Not to mention what they had been doing to earn their money.

Paul had always had a healthy respect for sex and believed it should only happen between people who loved each other.

It certainly should not be happening for money, and these people, men and women alike, were then just using the cash to feed their alcoholism and drug habits. Paul could not understand it. He was appalled by these addictions and the weak people who succumbed to them.

A few years ago, he had decided to make it his 'mission' in life to tackle this problem. He set about cleaning up the streets of his city, one whore at a time.

Parking his pedicab Paul walked the last half a block and snuck through the hole in the fence he had discovered when he first followed the women home.

As he expected there was only one there. They always left one to look after their few meagre possessions while the other two went out to work the streets. As usual the one left behind was drunk and had fallen asleep propped up against the dumpster they used as a shelter.

It didn't take Paul long to administer the needle with the anaesthetic in it and go back and get his pedicab, drawing it alongside the hole in the wire fence surrounding the warehouse. He lifted the blonde woman through the hole and into the cab gently. Then carefully arranging her as though she was dozing in the back of his cab. Paul pulled down the rain curtain and tucked a blanket around her legs so she would be warm.

He turned back and left a plastic bag he had brought with him next to the dumpster. It contained a box of Kleenex, toothbrushes and a tube of toothpaste. He'd added some baby wipes, fresh fruit, a loaf of bread, cheese and four bottles of water. Hopefully the other two women would eat the healthy food and use the toiletries he had provided for them. He would try to get back to them later next week, if he could.

Paul had long ago accepted that he wouldn't be able to help them all, only a select few would be able to join him as family members but he prided himself on making every effort to treat everyone equally and with care, love and respect.

Once Paul had arrived home again he quietly wheeled his pedicab inside, unlocked the servants' quarters and took the woman into his work room. He was careful not to turn the lights on until he had fully closed the door. With the windows blacked out, as they were, no light would show as he went about his business until well into the night.

While he worked, Paul liked to listen to classical music. He found it calmed him and it was part of what he liked to call his 'passing on ritual' for the people he helped. He had a routine and after switching on some soft Vivaldi and gloving up he set about disrobing his guest and cleaning her body, brushing her hair and doing her teeth. He manicured her nails and payed particular attention to cleaning her face. He had become quite adept at women's grooming practices, able to wax eyebrows and cleanse, tone and moisturise. He could apply basic makeup and even give a reasonable hair cut when required. He had taught himself how to use a hair straightener, do a blow wave and understood the importance of conditioning.

All the while he worked on this poor woman he spoke in soothing tones, explaining how she was extra special and had been chosen to join his family. He explained how she should appreciate his dedicating his life to providing a warm, nurturing environment for people like her to make the transition from this world to the next.

He would let them listen to beautiful music. Sometimes he would put on the television and tune it to a channel with nature programs or equally calming or informative shows.

He would remind them that although they had fallen from grace by turning to alcohol, drugs, prostitution and other crimes he was there now to help them repent for their sins.

It was his job to prepare them, both mentally and physically to finally meet the Lord and help move them into heaven to do Gods' work up there.

Often, he would turn on the CD player he had set up with an eBook and it would read to them passages from the bible while he busied himself pampering his guest.

Paul had his own mental image of God that had begun when he was a five-year-old orphan in the convent.

It had been shaped and honed over the years as he was being transferred from one foster home to another until at the age of eleven he eventually escaped the system and took refuge in a little church in the middle of South Carolina.

He had lived in a tiny room off the vestry, putting up with the noise and lack of privacy, enduring the sick demands of the priest in charge of the small congregation in this little country town. In return he received food and shelter from the man of God and a basic education. Paul would creep into the office each night after the priest had finished with him and study for hours on the church computer. He learned to read and appreciate the arts, he taught himself mathematics and progressed to harder subjects as the years passed.

During the day, he managed to become a skilled handyman at the church. He would do jobs for local parishioners too. Just before his nineteenth birthday he finally decided to take charge of his life and proceeded to enforce his version of God's will upon the priest. Paul punished him relentlessly for two days in the cellar under the manse. Finally he let him die and move on to meet his maker, where he would answer for the inexcusable sins against Paul and other young boys in the community.

"There you go my lovely lady," Paul finished up with the woman he had brought home and stood back to admire his handiwork.

She looked beautiful, even if he did say so himself. She was completely docile now, occasionally dozing off, in and out of consciousness. When the small dose of Ketamine he'd injected had worn off he had given her his own concoction of Diphenhydramine and other Rohypnol based drugs. His Conscience Cocktail he liked to call it. He had experimented a lot over the years before coming up with his own version of an effective neuromuscular blocking drug.

Researching sedatives, human paralysis, and although there had been four or five cases of his guests leaving this world a little earlier than he had planned, very early in the piece, he had refined the cocktail to such an extent he rarely had any adverse reactions. His guests never feeling any pain, or waking up too much or too quickly.

Paul had efficiently washed and trimmed her hair, giving her some wavy curls using the blow dryer. He had scrubbed every inch of her body, realising she was a lot younger than he first thought. A hard life, like the one she had obviously had to endure, would do that to a person. He had applied moisturiser and a light coating of make-up, trimmed and painted her finger and toe nails a nice subtle pink and dressed her in a new pale blue modest dress with white Mary Janes.

He regularly ordered a range of what he considered to be respectable clothes and shoes in a variety of sizes from the internet so he never had to go into shops to purchase the necessities.

Although occasionally he'd spend time looking through the windows of some of the bigger stores to ensure he was keeping up with trends.

Over the years he had become adept at estimating a woman's dress, panty or shoe size. Although he had only a limited supply of make-up, he was pretty sure he managed to match their skin tones and apply appropriate eye shadow and a swipe of blush to enhance their natural beauty.

Paul sat his guest in the chair he had designed and set up in front of the small television on the second floor of the servants' quarters. It had soft, padded restraints and it was made of quality leather. It tilted back at the top, ever so slightly, ensuring his guests heads would never loll forward and they would always feel comfortable.

He spent a few moments tucking a rug around her legs, making sure she had an uninterrupted view of the television before he took a few 'happy snaps' for the family album.

"Ok, I have to go now but I've made you comfortable so you just sit there and watch television, get some rest, and take this time to think about all your sins. I will be back tomorrow and we will plan your part in Julie's transition ceremony together." Paul gently patted the woman's hair and left, taking time to clean up his work area, his tools and the workbench before he turned out the lights and locked up for the night. He was happy he had been able to rescue this woman from her intolerable life and would soon be welcoming her into his family and his home. In a couple of months he would help her move into her 'forever home' with the Lord.

It didn't take him long to shower and change for bed, then he spent the next twenty minutes chatting with his family about his new girlfriend and the plan for the ceremony tomorrow.

Kissing his family goodnight and snuggling in tight to Julie, he whispered "Love you honey," and proceeded to sleep peacefully until the alarm woke him up at 8am.

Paul had always been able to sleep well, which he attributed to living a good, clean life, respecting others, doing his charity work and caring for his family. He spent all his waking hours taking care of others, thinking of others and trying to better the world, one task at a time. He considered himself a simple man, with simple needs. He didn't long for money, possessions or accolades, obtaining his gratification and satisfaction from knowing the work he had committed his life to would be his legacy to the world. If pressed to describe the feeling he would probably have said he had always felt a need to have a family to take care of, ever since he was a young boy and had lost his own 'real' family to a freak accident.

He tried not to think too much of the horrible night when storms had sent a huge tree through the living room window and wiped out his mother, father and big sister. God had indeed challenged him, given him hurdles to overcome and had ultimately developed him into the person he was now. As a small child, he had looked at the accident as some sort of punishment, and the life he had to live after that was payback for having survived when the rest of his family had perished.

However, when he had occasion to visit a lawyer for a small indiscretion when he was twenty-two he had discovered, purely by chance, he had a trust fund.

This had been set up for him by the insurance company his family had in place and due to his being lost in the system for many years. The money had been invested on his behalf, wisely it seemed, and was payable to him upon his having reached his twenty-first birthday. Paul had taken his 'inheritance' and with it he had begun his quest to have a family to look after, and then, years later he started his extra charity work, saving those poor lost souls and assisting them to transcend to a better place where they could do the Lord's work.

"Morning my love," Paul gave Julie a cuddle and then spent the next hour dressing her for the day. "It's a very special time for us now sweetheart. This is what we have planned for this past eight weeks. Today is your transition day." Paul couldn't help but feel excited. These were the days that made everything he did worthwhile.

They were what he worked towards and he felt a sense of pride knowing his beautiful Julie would soon be heading off to be with God and to continue his work in heaven.

He placed Julie by the window so she could look out at the creamy white magnolia flowers in bloom on the porch, while he attended to everyone else. He took his time today, he wanted everyone looking especially well dressed, in their Sunday best as it were, for Julie's special day. Mom and Dad were fine. His two sisters took a little longer, with their make-up and their hair. He had a little glitch with his kid brother, something he hadn't been expecting. Lately he had noticed young Harry was looking a lot paler than the rest of his family and he had seen him having tremors yesterday.

Now it appeared that Harry had passed away during the night. Paul chastised himself for not anticipating this. He had worried about the boy because he was so young. He had never had a brother or sister under the age of fifteen before, but when he had found his sister she had a four-year-old boy with her.

At first, he didn't even consider her for his family, but after watching them for several weeks he had realised this poor boy had been subjected to situations no child should ever have to endure. He and his mother were perfect candidates for Paul's family. He was going to be able to help both of them. What a bonus!

Paul spent the afternoon preparing the cocktails his family would 'consume' at the ceremony this evening and he took a quick trip over to the Walgreens on Decatur Street for a few extra bits and pieces he needed. he set up the sofa and brought in the dining chairs, re-arranging the living room so there was plenty of space for everyone. They all faced the two modified antique chairs he brought up from the basement. He looked them over admiringly. After the fiasco a few years ago when he had underestimated the quantity of sodium thiopental he required for the transition ceremony and one of his beloved family was injured when they woke up from their paralysed state, he had made some changes to the entire ceremony.

He had modelled his transition ceremony on the lethal injection system, where they generally use a combination of three drugs; Sodium thiopental as an anesthetic to induce unconsciousness, pancuronium bromide to cause muscle paralysis and respiratory arrest, and potassium chloride to stop the heart.

However, as Paul found out in 2002 it was drastically important to get just the right quantities into the body in the right order.

Not enough sodium thiopental reacting in time, before the other two, meant the body was racked with horrible convulsions. Naturally Paul wanted to minimise the pain and distress to his guests and family members as much as possible.

The new chairs were elegant, padded and he had special restraints, made with a beautiful soft velvet fabric, that slipped over their body, legs and arms God forbid anything untoward would ever happen again during the ceremony.

Glancing at the clock Paul realised he had a little more time than he thought. Everything was in order for the ceremony and his family were already in their places. He smiled, thinking this would be the perfect opportunity to say his personal goodbyes and show his gratefulness to Julie for being his girlfriend these past few weeks. He would spend the next hour giving her one of his special loving massages and then they could shower and change for the ceremony in time for the 7pm start. He quickly undressed and snuck into the bedroom, closing the door for privacy.

By 6.45pm Paul and Julie were ready He had showered and put on his suit as he always did. He like to think it brought a sense of formality to the proceedings. He placed Julie on her chair, resplendent in her bridal gown with the new little shoulder length veil. It had been unfortunate his last girlfriend had been a bleeder and the blood stain just wouldn't come out of the old, floor length veil he had used for nearly six years.

He had decided to purchase a new, slightly more accommodating bridal gown when he had ordered the veil online. It hadn't been too expensive and it looked like it was going to suit about four or five different sizes as it was a nice big A-line, with a matching belt that could cinch in the waist if required.

He brought the guest in from the servants' quarters and gave her pride of place in the large recliner he usually reserved for his dad. He made sure everyone was comfortable and then started his ceremony.

After reading a few passages from the bible and making his usual speech thanking both Harry and Julie for their devotion to the family Paul picked up the book of names from the coffee table.

He took it over to Julie and closing his eyes he used her hand to flip the pages, finally picking one and running her finger down to a name on the list. "Glenda," he exclaimed. "Thank you, Julie, you have done a great job."

He then slowly, carefully gave her the three injections. With a loving kiss to the top of her head and a ruffling of young Harry's hair he turned and took his seat on the arm of the recliner next to his new girlfriend 'Glenda'. He liked to spend the next twenty minutes or so in prayer, and presumed his family would use the quiet time to do the same.

After taking the usual pictures for the family album the whole ceremony was over by 7.45pm. Paul spent the next hour preparing his family for the evening, putting away their dress shoes, hanging their formal wear in the home-made closets in the basement and redressing them in their normal, everyday clothing.

He took a quick timeout to heat a frozen dinner and eat it with Glenda, explaining the process that would now take place. He returned her to the rearranged living room with the rest of the family. Sitting her right next to the window in the middle of the love seat, central to the rest of the gang. It would be good for her to spend some time alone with them, in this, the 'getting to know you' phase of their relationship. He took his time cleaning equipment and returning it to his workshop. He removed Julie's body and carefully undressed it, wrapping it in some cheap material he kept for this purpose. It occurred to Paul that it was a waste of time and effort, not to mention clothing, to fully dress them again. The soul had now departed, joining its Maker and this was just a clean-up operation now.

Julie's body was put into a black, heavy duty, jumbo bin liner bag. For Harry it was much quicker, he had no shoes on, his outfit was simple to remove and he barely had to use a third of the material he'd used on Julie. There was no need for modesty or special treatment, although he liked to think he was still gentle, and took care not to scrape the bodies against a wall or bang them into furniture when he carried them into the servants' quarters. They would remain there until Paul got up early in the morning to take them to the cabin.

The only exception to this ritual were his dads. He believed it was a sign of respect for them to be transported fully dressed so over the years he had always left their clothes on, choosing to burn them at the time of the body disposal.

He often puzzled as to whether this was some sort of symbolism…the father, the head of the house, deserving of special treatment.

Or perhaps it was just that it had always been a little harder for him to come to terms with having to wash and dress his parents, especially his dads, more than his sisters, brothers or girlfriends.

He understood how the Lord had chosen him for this work and he must never question His ways, but he still had a tiny bit of discomfort when having to tend to his naked parents.

Paul finally finished up around 10pm and headed off for his first night with Glenda. He always took it slow with his new girlfriends as he was not the sort of man to rush into things. Nor did he derive any pleasure from feeling like he was forcing people to do things they were uncomfortable with. After a quick kiss he rolled over and faced the wall, closing his eyes he spent just a moment saying a final goodnight to Julie under his breath.

The alarm woke him at 2am. Although still a little tired from his busy day yesterday Paul knew it was important to get started on his clean-up work early. After dressing in his night work gear and adding a black beanie and gloves he headed over to the mid-city storage unit for the truck.

He locked his pedicab inside the unit, drove the truck back to the quarter and loaded his cargo in the back, covering the back securely with an old painter's tarp.

He gathered the sandwiches he'd prepared, his duffle bag and headed out to the bayou where he, Julie and Harry would spend the rest of the night together before he loaded them into their cage and fed the 'gators.

45

As he turned on to North Rampart, out of sight of his home, he hadn't seen the red fire engine pull up, or the flashing lights from the police vehicle but he shivered, like someone had walked over his grave.

"Ok sir, so you say there is a burst water pipe in your servants' quarters, and when you knocked on your neighbor's door to warn him about the leaking water you got concerned." The New Orleans Police Department (NOPD) cop was both mature and experienced and handled the old man with care. Ritchie had called in the emergency about forty minutes ago, just after 3pm, saying that although he had called the fire department and they were on their way to look at the burst pipe he was now concerned about his neighbor, Paul.

"Yes sir. I was very worried about the water getting into Paul's place next door. I know he uses the back condo to preserve flowers, or fruit, or furniture or something."

"I didn't want the darn pipe to ruin his equipment. I went over to his place and knocked on the door, a few times." Ritchie mimed knocking loudly on the door

"I knocked loudly because I could see a lamp on in the front room and the drapes weren't quite closed. I saw someone sitting in a chair watching TV. My eyesight sure isn't the best, so I couldn't see if it was Paul, or one of his family, but there is certainly someone in the front room." Ritchie paused to take a sip of water from a bottle on the side table. "Anyways, I called out, and banged on the door, then the window, but I didn't get any answer. Now I'm not just concerned about the water leak, what if there is something else wrong?"

"Well sir, we are just going to have to check on Mr Paul and his family then aren't we."

"What's Paul's last name Mr Gordon? And who are the members of his family?" the old policeman asked.

"Well, that's kinda strange," Ritchie replied. "I don't think I have ever heard Paul mention his last name. I know he lives there with his girlfriend, and his folks, his mom and his dad I believe. Then there's a sister, maybe a brother. Gracious me, what a poor neighbor I must be to not even know his family, their names or anything."

"Don't you worry about it Mr Gordon. That's the way of the world nowadays. Half of us wouldn't even know if we had a serial killer living next door, we're too busy with our own lives," he chuckled.

"We will just head in next door and do a quick 'welfare check', make sure everyone is ok, and we will be sure to tell Mr Paul about the water pipe and possible leakage into his back condo."

"Come on officer, lets head over there now. We will pop back in before we leave just to reassure you everything is fine. Mr Gordon, don't you worry. Can I get you anything before we go?"

"No, thank you. I do appreciate this Sergeant. I don't usually pry or like to be a bother to people so I am grateful for your time. If all is fine I will feel silly, worrying for nothing, but you never know, do you?"

"That's exactly right. Better to err on the side of caution." the policeman said as he was leaving. "What do you think William? Anything to worry about?" the old cop asked his young partner as they left and headed over to the neighbor's house.

"Nope, just some old geezer stressing about nothing. Probably woke up and freaked over the water leak. The family next door is more than likely sleeping through the whole thing, completely oblivious."

And with that he opened the front gate, strode up to the door and knocked loudly, calling out "Police! We're here for a welfare check sir, please open the door."

After getting no response, he tried again. A little louder this time and using his fist to knock.

The sergeant wandered across to the window, noting the drapes had a gap in the middle and they seemed to be caught up on something just inside the window.

As his eyes adjusted to the darkness inside he could start to make out the shape of a recliner, a television, a coffee table and there was a darkish shape. It looked like someone slightly slumped over, perhaps fallen asleep, in the chair in front of the TV. He took another look at the drapes.

Suddenly the old sergeant sprung back from the window, drawing his weapon and motioning Will aside. He put his finger to his lips in the universal sign to keep quiet and whispered "Something wrong here. I can feel it. We're going in Will."

Sergeant Jones took a couple of steps back, dropped his left shoulder and prepared to take a run at the front door. "Hang on Sarge," his partner instructed him. "I'll do that, you're going to do your shoulder in if you do it!"

Officer William Anderson had only been with the NOPD for little more than a year so he was still a bit gung-ho when it came to some situations, but the older sergeant was more than happy on this occasion to let him do the grunt work.

He stood to the side of Will and raised his weapon slightly. "Ok son, do it," he directed.

The young officer though lithe and fit took three attempts before the door finally busted off its hinges. As soon as they entered the hallway he realised immediately why Anderson had not been able to simply break the lock. He could see the door still attached to the frame by three separate deadlocks.

"Slowly," Jones instructed the young officer, "I'll go first."

They crept down the hall, spotting a kitchen to the back, a closed door they presumed was a bedroom to the right and the front room on the left. Jones, weapon extended, proceeded to enter the living room and flicked on the light switch by the door. The first thing to hit them was the smell. Later they would both have trouble describing it exactly. No exactly the same as de-comp, Jones would say, it was sicklier than that. It was like sweet smelling garbage.

It took a full three minutes, standing there, silently dumfounded, before the horror set in. The old sergeant took one look at his young partner and grabbed his shirt, dragging the kid out of the house. Anderson stumbled out the gate and walked to the corner, before he finally threw up. Sergeant Jones proceeded to pull out his radio and shakily ask command for back up.

"Suspected umm, well, suspected.... I don't know, but something bad has gone down at this address." The old cop was looking a bit white and shaken now and William couldn't stop heaving. Neither of them could make head nor tail of what they had just seen.

"Immediate back up requested, send two cars, no, make it three. Actually, I think the Captain might even need to get involved with this one. You better send a bus too, no, make that three ambulances and some medics. I think I counted about five of them in there."

"Five of what sir? Are there dead bodies, are there injured persons?" The dispatcher wanted to know the details.

"I...I....I just don't know. Sorry. I don't know what they are. Just send some help for god's sakes," and he signed off, slid down the wall and slumped over, tears flowing from his eyes.

It was just after 10.30am when Paul had finished returning the truck to the storage unit. He usually went straight to the car wash and detailed it before parking it back in its hidey hole, but the car wash had been closed with a sign saying it was undergoing repairs. Not to worry, he would go home and find the address of another one and pop back there tomorrow to give it a thorough clean.

He was just too tired today, and he was eager to return to the family. It seemed he was just so busy lately he had not had time to just sit and enjoy their company. He must make more of an effort.

Paul pulled the pedicab up next to the side gate, he then unlocked it and proceeded to cover it with a tarpaulin. He was returning to the gate to chain it up when it swung open. Lights flooded the courtyard, people rushed at him from the servant's quarters, through the gate, even from inside his house!*Good Lord*, he thought, *what the hell is going on.* "Stop!" he shouted. "What's going on? Where's my family? Has anything happened to them?"

Two men dressed in what he presumed was SWAT riot gear threw Paul to the ground. He must have counted at least fifteen different police, detectives, guys with all sorts of badges, in the backyard. He lay face down on the tiny patch of dirt next to the magnolia tree in the courtyard repeating his question over and over "Is my family ok? What's happened? Is everyone alright?"

The investigation and the ensuing court case went on for nearly thirteen weeks. A task force of over fifty detectives, police and investigators across three states got involved before the truth finally came out about the extent of Pauls' reign of terror. It appeared that Paul, born Henry Terrance Paul Fredrickson in Cincinnati Ohio thirty-nine years ago had a traumatic childhood. After losing his parents when he was young, he had been rotated through various foster homes and finally landed in a public orphanage. As an adult, they had traced his movements across three states and had now tied him to forty-two murders.

It would have been a nearly impossible task if it weren't for the family albums and journals Paul had kept so methodically in his basement. The inexperienced officer who had first discovered them had presumed they were just family keepsakes and hadn't realised the importance of the find. He had not immediately noticed that all the photos inside were of people who looked quite natural, but were in fact paralysed and had been posed for every photograph.

Each person, totally unrelated, had spent differing amounts of time as Paul's 'family' over the years. What had finally caught the policeman's eye was that one face always remained the same.

51

Paul was in every single photograph, even though the families were made up of many different people.

The newspapers had a field day of course. Reporting, then rehashing the details of the cocktails Paul used to keep his family drugged and interviewing, then re-interviewing old Ritchie and the staff at the café across the road. The biggest piece of the puzzle, discovered after the water pipe burst, and the catalyst to set the entire investigation in motion, was accredited to the faithful old policeman. Sergeant Jones had been doing his job yes, but he was an attentive cop, always being aware, looking for anything 'outside the box'.

For it was his keen eye that noticed the gap in the curtains. When interviewed by the Times-Picayune he related how at first everything had appeared ordinary, a hard-working guy fallen asleep in a chair in front of the TV, a lamp glowing in the corner, the living room looked normal, like thousands of living rooms all over New Orleans.

It was when he took a closer look at the curtain itself and realised the gap in the drapes had been caused by the material getting snagged by what looked like a bluish colored finger. That's when he knew something wasn't right. He knew they needed to get into the house right away.

When he and officer Anderson turned the living room light on and saw all those people sitting, posed, around the room, his first thought was that they had entered a film set.

These were mannequins or life like dolls being used in a movie. It wasn't until his gaze rested on the girl with the bridal veil, sitting by the window, that he slowly started to comprehend. Her hand was raised awkwardly, at a strange angle to her left and a finger had caught on the drapes.

He had stepped towards her. He'd looked into her eyes then and it was at that moment the horror hit him, for in the corner of this 'mannequin's' eye was a tiny tear, which then proceeded to roll slowly down her cheek to her chin.

What is a Villanelle?

A villanelle is a nineteen-line poem consisting of five, three line verses followed by a quatrain (four line verse). There are two refrains and two repeating rhymes, with the first and third line of the first verse repeated alternately until the last stanza, which includes both repeated lines.

In layman's terms the villanelle is an example of a fixed verse poem. It started as a simple ballad-like song, imitating peasant songs. Despite its French origins, the majority of villanelles have been written in English, a trend which began in the late nineteenth century. The villanelle has been noted as a form of poetry that frequently treats the subject of obsessions. Due to their lyrical nature and being considered a non-conventional style, villanelles often appealed to 'outsiders', songwriters or non-poetry writers.

Famous villanelles and their poets include:

Dylan Thomas – Do not go gentle into that good night

Theodore Roethke – The Waking

Jean Passerat – J'ay perdu ma Tourterelle

(I have lost my turtledove)

A Grove of Money Trees

I once saw a grove of money trees
Growing many a dollar bill
Fluttering and swaying in the breeze

Grabbing a bag, I dropped to my knees
Heartbeat so fast I would need a pill
I once saw a grove of money trees

I didn't want to be a sleaze
But I heard cash ringing like a till
Fluttering and swaying in the breeze

I was nearly done then heard a sneeze
Shock going through me, I felt a chill
I once saw a grove of money trees

The little girl spoke, making me freeze
"Can I have some too, Daddy is ill"
Fluttering and swaying in the breeze

"Take this bag home honey, take it please"
I stuffed more in, till it had its fill
I once saw a grove of money trees
Fluttering and swaying in the breeze

My 'Golden' Age

I awoke one day and I suddenly felt old
How to fix this problem, I couldn't think
The years are passing – they say my age is 'gold'

My bones didn't ache in heat or the cold
No sunspots and my hair black as ink
I awoke one day and I suddenly felt old

When on earth did these wrinkles take hold?
It seemed to happen, quick as a blink
The years are passing – they say my age is 'gold'

Aging gracefully – I am not sold
Aching joints and body parts that sink
I awoke one day and I suddenly felt old

Wisdom is gained, or so I am told
But forgetting is making me drink
The years are passing – they say my age is 'gold'

So near the end, not ready to fold
I don a glitter tutu that's pink
I awoke one day and I suddenly felt old
The years are passing – but I'm breaking the mould.

Bushfire

He turned to look. Like the heat from the bushfire flames his body began to warm up from the inside. The tingling grew and crept down to his loins and out along each limb as he took in the sight and he heard the first sirens start to scream through the night.

Oh my God, he shuddered, their noise is like an orchestral crescendo. He took a few minutes longer to stand and absorb the atmosphere.

From his vantage point here on the ridge he could see the glow of the fire and although it was difficult to make out the individual dancing flames, the glow was superb. A 'sun hot' yellow at the ground, radiating to an orange, a 'burnt' orange, he snickered at his own poor excuse for a joke, then finally that beautiful 'fire red'. From there the air turned black, then grey and lightening to an 'ash' colour out towards the periphery. A real artist's canvas he thought to himself. He listened to the background noise. The crackling, branches snapping and a cacophony of sirens from the ambulances, fire trucks and police. These were interspersed with the occasional shouts from the fire fighters and even a few squeals of birds and small animals as they fled the inferno that was engulfing their homes.

Ok, it was time to get going now. He took one last, lingering snapshot in his mind's eye, hoisted his backpack and trekked the final half a kilometre to where he had hidden his vehicle, in the thick copse just a few hundred metres from the fire's access road.

The radio was squawking continuously as men and women checked in, barked out their locations, asked for instructions or requested back up. A staging command post had been set up just two kilometres from where Mark's vehicle was parked so he radioed in as soon as he reached the truck.

"6-SKP, this is 6-SKP requesting instructions. I've just finished my break in Boddington, where would you like me to go command centre?" He sat patiently in his fire vehicle's cab, waiting for an answer. As he risked another look in the rear-view mirror and marvelled at the magnificent scene of devastation behind him his radio came to life.

"6-SKP this is command centre. Request you proceed to fire access road one kilometre east of the South West Highway at Boddington. Please notify us on your arrival. Be aware, possible arsonist still in the area, be vigilant. Thanks 6-SKP. Command centre out."

He could not help but smile to himself. Possible arsonist? Hardly. He was a *definite* arsonist, and a damn good one too, even if he did say so himself. He went on proudly, I mean, how many others could say they had lit twenty-three successful fires in a nine-month period, *and* helped put them all out! He had a perfect record.

Jumping out of the cab he removed the accelerant bottles from his backpack with his gloved hands. He placed them carefully on some dry bracken and cleared a small 'moat' around the pile. Adding his gloves to the mound he took his lighter and ignited a small twig, placing it into the leaves under the bottles and watched as the flame quickly took hold. Mark grinned, nothing like it in this world, that feeling of controlling a fire....

Pieces of Eight

"Pieces of eight, pieces of eight," that's what it sounded like the parrot was saying. But maybe that was my romantic notions taking over. After all, I was on a beautiful white beach, next to a clear, sparkling blue lagoon. Miles from anywhere on a tropical island. The parrot was perched upon a gnarly old salt, wearing old fashioned sailors garb and peering through a telescope at a boat moored just off shore.

"Pieces of eight, pieces of eight," the parrot squawked again. I sipped my Margarita and closed my eyes.

"MOM! Can I please have a piece of cake?" my daydream was suddenly shattered by my daughters' high pitched voice. "Good grief Mom, were you asleep? It's the middle of the day!" She giggled.

Obviously, I had dozed off, just for a minute I'm sure, while sitting in front of the window that looked out on the busy street below. With the sun shining through and touching my face my mind had wandered into a fantasy land I often dreamed about...Carefree Island – my affectionate name for it. I smiled to myself. A place to retreat to, in my daydreams, where there were no cares or worries, where I didn't have to work two part-time jobs to make ends meet. There was no bum of an ex-husband there, forever asking me for money. There was no landlord constantly griping about rent control and refusing to fix the slightest thing that goes wrong.

"Sure honey, not too large a slice now, dinner is only a couple of hours away."

I picked myself up and busied myself washing up the dirty coffee cup, tidying away the cake and knife Jules had left on the bench and preparing the casserole to go in the oven for dinner.

"How was school Jules? Did you get your result back for the Maths test?" I called to my daughter who had taken her cake to the dining table and was sitting doing her homework, while sipping a glass of homemade lemon cordial.

"Not yet, probably Tuesday. Oh, and Mrs Kennedy said to say hi, she was picking up Jonathon as I was walking home. I need $2 for a sausage sizzle to raise funds for the homeless on Friday too, and the zipper broke on my pencil case so I need a new one, sorry Mom."

I am mighty proud of my beautiful daughter Julie Marie Strickland. At twelve years old she is so wise, so thoughtful, so caring. She never complains about how tough things are, never asks for anything she doesn't absolutely need and has a heart as big as an elephant.

I finished the casserole, popped it in the oven and went to get the laundry in from the balcony, stooping to kiss Jules on the head as I went past.

"That's fine honey. I will pick up a pencil case tomorrow at the store, and leave you the $2 on the table for your sausage sizzle. How is Jonathon? Is he still a bit keen on you?"

Continuing outside, I knew full well that Jules would be blushing uncontrollably now. I smiled to myself again. After bringing in the washing, folding and putting away it was time to check on the casserole.

"Oh, did you bring in the mail Jules?" I asked my daughter, spying an envelope on the little hall table just inside the front door of our apartment.

"Yeah, there was just one letter for you, I put it on the table. I finished my homework ma, can I go to my room and listen to some music while I read?"

"Sure," I answered distractedly, opening the envelope while walking to the kitchen.

Dear Mrs Williams, the letter began, I regret to inform you that your god-mother, Mrs Jacinta Haldon, of 3 Cassowary Close, Grenadine, Mississippi, has passed away. She left a last will and testament, in which you were named as a beneficiary. Mrs Haldon has bequeathed you an item of intrinsic value (notional financial value noted) and this has been sent to you by courier and should arrive within the week. We are very sorry for your loss. Should we be able to assist you any further please do not hesitate to call our office. Regards Jack Kellerman, Attorney-at-law.

I sat myself down on the chair by the window. That's a bit of a bolt out of the blue. It must be nearly twenty-five years since I had seen 'Aunt Jacinta'. She was the lovely old lady who looked after me every day after school so that my mother could work at the diner to support us.

I loved going to her house…even though she had been a strict taskmaster. Not having children of her own she had welcomed the opportunity to look after me and although my mother often bought her a bag of groceries, or a packet of handkerchiefs, she never accepted payment of any money.

She had made me sit and do my homework every afternoon, often making me read when I had no reading homework – secretly I always believed that was because she had such poor eyesight and loved having me read to her.

She had always followed this with homemade cake or slice, or my favourite, pecan cookies and big glasses of fresh orange juice or homemade lemonade, a tradition I had passed on to my daughter.

A tear snaked its way down my cheek. I was overcome with guilt for not keeping in contact, although it really would have been difficult after we moved to New York twenty-two years ago.

I wonder what had happened to her? The letter didn't really say, although it didn't indicate anything untoward, so, by my calculations she would have been about eighty-seven years old, meaning that perhaps it was just her time. I stood up and wiped the tear from my eye, what a lovely old soul I thought. Putting the letter on the pile of filing in the drawer of the desk in the kitchen I pondered about the item she had left me. I didn't even have to think about it really. My favourite thing at Aunt Jacinta's had been the little brooch that Aunt used to wear all through the winter. She loved to wear scarves and she would have this brooch pinned to a scarf once or twice a week. It was in the shape of a fat little bird and so cute, and I never tired of hearing the story she used to tell about it.

Apparently, when her mother, Helen, was a young girl she had belonged to a tennis club, and after she had been playing for about a year this boy called Jacob joined the club and he really took her eye. He was polite and courteous and called her ma'am and always held the door open for her.

It took him about three months before he finally worked up the courage to ask her to join him for a lemon squash, one day after a particularly exhausting game of tennis. Well, from that day things blossomed and he courted her over the next eighteen months.

Finally, one day she arrived at the club to play a game of tennis, supposedly a foursome with friends, and she discovered him waiting in the club rooms, down on one knee, with ten of their best friends surrounding him. He proposed to her right there and gave her a beautiful ring and three months later they were married. Well, her lovely beau was a kind, generous man, but unfortunately, he was also extremely sickly, and just eleven months into their marriage he passed away of a terrible ailment. Aunt Jacinta's mother was heartbroken.

Theirs was a once in a lifetime love, he treasured her and called her his hummingbird and she doted on him with all her heart. A few weeks after he passed she found out she was pregnant with his child.

She had always told Jacinta that she was sure her father, had planned this, along with everything else, as he was the most efficient, organised man she knew. He had even planned a one-year anniversary present, knowing that he would probably not be there to give it to her.

Helen had received a letter in the mail from a solicitor a week before their wedding anniversary saying that Jacob had made a reservation for dinner for her at a lovely restaurant – their favourite, in the local neighbourhood. She was instructed that she should attend this reservation at 7pm, so she did.

Upon arriving at the restaurant, she found it filled with her and Jacob's friends, all of whom had received instructions to be there to help her through this tough time without him. Of course, she could let them all know then that she was pregnant with his child. They celebrated together, the meal and drinks all pre-paid by Jacob before he had passed away.

At the end of the night the owner of the restaurant came up to Helen and presented her with a little gift, wrapped beautifully in silver paper with a black bow. He informed her that Jacob had left this gift several months before, with instructions that he give it to her on this night.

Upon opening the paper Helen was overwhelmed to see a beautiful brooch in the shape of a bird with a shiny stone for his eye. The note read... To my darling Helen, I know the times ahead are going to be tough, but you are strong like an eagle, I know the times ahead will sometimes be sad, but you bring joy to those around you like a bright coloured parakeet, I know the times ahead will bring much turmoil for you, but you are like a turtle dove, bringing peace to all who know you...you are my love, my precious humming bird and I will watch over you and our offspring from above, forever.

I wiped away the tears that were rolling down my cheek. I had always loved that story, and believed that it was from remembering that little bird brooch that my tropical island dreams stemmed.

They always involved a bird of some sort, either swooping albatross, seagulls screeching overhead, pelicans waddling along the sands, mysterious toucans in the palm trees, or, like today, a parrot perched on a sailor's shoulder.

I certainly hoped that the item my Aunt had so thoughtfully left to me would be that beautiful little brooch. I had remembered her saying many times that she felt the brooch had 'watched over her' since she had received it, like it had watched over her mother many years ago.

Shifting my thoughts back to the present I called to Jules that dinner was ready and hurried to set the table for the two of us. I would just have to wait till the courier arrived with the parcel to discover what I had been left by my favourite aunt.

Wednesday afternoon had dragged. It had been blustery when I finally left the diner and made my way to the bus for the twenty-minute journey home. I'd spent the morning giving the pantry at work a thorough clean. The afternoon shift had three of us rostered on, but because of the unseasonably cool, windy weather the diner had been awfully quiet, about five customers over three hours. I was glad to be heading home. I picked up some fresh milk and two apples at the corner store before heading up the four flights of stairs to the apartment. Arriving at the landing I saw a man in a uniform about to knock on my door.

"Hello? Are you looking for me?" I asked him.

"Are you Francis Williams? If so, then yes, I have a parcel for you," he replied.

"That's me. Just let me put the bags down," and I opened my door, placing the shopping and my work bag on the little table we use in the entryway. "Just sign here ma'am," the courier pointed to an electronic pad and handed me what looked like a metal pencil. I duly signed his e-docket and he handed over a small, envelope sized parcel.

I couldn't wait to get inside and realised as the door slammed I hadn't even said thank you! "Thanks," I called out to the closed door, making my way to my favourite spot – the chair by the window in the kitchen that overlooks the magnificent New York City skyline – the reason we took this apartment eight years ago. I sat and looked the parcel over.

It had my name and address on the front, and a bar code of some sort. On the back were the sender's details: J. Kellerman, Kellerman and Sons, Attorneys-at-law. 16 Penn Avenue, Natchez, Mississippi. It was certainly the right package then.

Tentatively I unwrapped the first layer, the outer wrapping was simple brown paper, followed by a double layer of white paper, a thin cardboard, then a thick layer of bubble wrap.

Goodness, they were thorough. Perhaps it's not the brooch, perhaps it's a little crystal ornament or something instead? But no, as I turned over the final layer of bubble wrap there it was, nestled in the wrapping like a bird in a nest. The brooch sat and glistened, the little eye sparkling at me. My heart melted and tears flowed as I cradled the brooch to my chest and gently rocked back and forward.

It was easily as beautiful as I remembered all those years ago. I was filled with love and respect mixed with a little sadness as I remembered Aunt Jacinta fondly. I could hear her voice though, saying *now don't you cry young lady, you just say thank you very much and then put a smile on your face!* I stood up to go to the sink to wash my face, placing the brooch on the counter, and as I did I realised that a tiny piece of paper was stuck to the bottom of the bird's claw.

I hadn't noticed it at first because it could only be seen from an angle. It was like a piece of tissue or something had got stuck in its little foot. I tried to brush it off, gently, but it just wouldn't budge. I went to the drawer and retrieved a pair of tweezers and ever so carefully tried to wiggle it out.

Suddenly the brooch seemed to spring apart! It startled me so much I literally jumped backwards, dropping the brooch on the bubble wrap on the counter.

I stepped forward to see if I had broken it and realised that the bird had opened, on a little hinge, like its tummy - I had always thought it was a fat little thing - was a secret compartment. It was only small, less than the size of a dime, slightly bigger than a nickel, but surprisingly deep, at least the depth of your little finger. Inside were tiny little shiny pieces of glass.

Not glistening exactly, more like bits of broken glass. And the folded piece of paper that I had seen the edge of as I had turned the brooch over. I lifted the paper out with the tweezers and unfolded it. Words were written in faded ink pen in a beautiful calligraphy.

My darling Helen, I love you with all my heart and I am so sorry we cannot be together longer. I have put these diamonds in here for you so that I can help support you and our child for the rest of your lives. Take a stone each year or so to our good friend Ralph and he will sell it, providing enough money for you both to live comfortably. Be strong my little hummingbird and we will meet again in heaven. Always your Jacob xxx

I could barely believe what I was reading. It was incredible. That wonderful man had provided for his wife and child in this beautiful brooch. Turning the paper over I read the words printed in modern pen in what was distinctly my Aunt Jacinta's old-fashioned hand writing.

My darling Francis, I have never been blessed with a child of my own but have always thought of you as a part of me. Thank you for all those years you gave me inspiration and comfort when I had lost my husband and was thinking I had nothing left to look forward to. Helping your mother to raise you gave me such joy and purpose. My mother gave me this brooch before she passed away and between us we have used just over half the stones my father left us.

I have kept in touch with your mother until she died and she kept me up to date with your achievements, especially your lovely daughter.

I want you and your beautiful Julie to have the rest of these stones and this brooch and hope that you will let me repay your kindness in this way. All my love Aunty Jacinta. Xxx

My hands shook as I placed the paper on the counter with the brooch and I slowly slid down the cupboard door to sit on the floor. Holding my head in my hands I sobbed. I sobbed for my mother, who all her life had struggled with alcoholism and had finally gone to heaven many years ago now, I sobbed for the lovely Aunt Jacinta and the hours I had spent with her.

I sobbed for Helen, who, like me, and my mother before me, had looked after her daughter all alone. And I sobbed for the amazing Jacob, who's legacy had helped, and was going to continue to help, over four generations of women.

When Jules got home and found me crying on the floor she rushed to my side. I reassured her that I was fine, and slowly I recounted the story of the bird brooch to her. It was dark by the time I finished and we still sat together on the kitchen floor, neither of us wanting to get up to turn on a light in case it broke this beautiful moment. I held my daughter in my arms as she too sobbed.

We were going to be ok. We were going to be supported by this wonderful legacy for the rest of our lives and we were grateful and respectful. We whispered our thanks to Jacob...

First Love

She arrived on my birthday, my twelfth to be exact.
The box was huge, it took a while to unpack.
But there she stood proud, I didn't know what to think,
she was shiny and new and pretty – and pink.
She took my breath away, my heart pounding so fast,
I couldn't imagine such a strong love would not last.

We spent six years together, inseparable, each day.
She fulfilled all my dreams, my hopes, in every way.
She made me laugh, she made me cry.
When we were together, wow! would we fly.
I didn't have time for boys, like Pete or Mike.
Coz she was my first love, my Malvern Star BIKE.

The Nun and the Gun

He didn't like to involve the sisters, but what else could he do? He'd staked out the compound for two days and couldn't see any other way.

"If there is any sign of trouble, or you feel uncomfortable you just abort the mission, leaving as you normally do. Ok?" Sampson waited for both nuns to nod their agreement. "Alright then, good luck."

"Oh, we won't need luck Mr Peters, God will be with us, every step of the way," said Sister Sofia, the younger of the two. Picking up their cart they headed up the street towards the Cobra's headquarters.

Diego Lopez, the leader of the cartel was away. The locals referred to him as serpiente loca or 'crazy snake'. Sampson would never have undertaken this rescue mission if Lopez had been in town. It was risky enough with just the meagre skeleton crew left behind.

Sampson watched the nuns push their cart up to the wrought iron gates in the cement wall. The Sisters had negotiated an arrangement with Lopez years ago. Weekly they would bring supplies from the marketplace. Stocking the cupboards, cooking and cleaning in return for the Cobra's leaving the Sisters in peace and 2000 pesos per week.

Once inside the gates Sampson put his revolver, snipers rifle and binoculars into a bag. He headed out to the jeep. He drove slowly not kicking up any dust, then turning onto the strip of bitumen running alongside the compound.

Investigations earlier had revealed a huge tree behind the compound that provided a good view of the interior buildings.

Sampson settled into the tree, prepared to wait until he knew the nuns were safely out again. There was little activity inside the walls. He could see a group of three men playing cards outside the bunkhouse, which housed the basement prison. The nuns' cart was at the kitchen, groceries unloaded, except for the box of liquor Sampson had organised. He watched as one of the men spied the box and wandered over, having a discussion with Sister Clarita, who threw him a filthy look and returned to the kitchen. The man took the tequila back to his posse who begun guzzling. Sampson smiled, *yes*, he thought, *that liquor was a good idea.*

For the next two hours, the men got louder and drunker. He saw the nuns moving about in the kitchen then cross to the bunkhouse. He grimaced when one man threw his arm around Sister Sofia and squeezed her buttocks.

An hour later the men had started to quieten down. Two had wandered to the hammocks and dozed off. The other was chatting with a fourth man who had been patrolling the interior of the compound earlier but had joined the others when he spotted the tequila. Both men were now leaning back in their chairs, feet up on the railing, eyes closed. Exactly as he had hoped. Sister Clarita came out of the building, glanced around and headed towards the kitchen. She put two empty dirty-linen bags into the cart, returned to the bunkhouse, taking the bags inside. Soon the nuns carried an obviously full, heavy bag out to the cart, returning inside for the second. This one was visibly lighter, they placed it on top and proceeded to push the cart towards the gates.

Suddenly one of the guards slipped from his chair. He woke with a start and saw the women preparing to leave so wandered over to them. Sister Clarita said something but he continued to walk towards them. Sister Sofia hastened to put herself between him and the cart, purposefully bending over in front of him to pick up something from the dirt. He saw the man smile, slap her on the bottom, laughing as she squealed. Sister Clarita opened the top bag and showed the man what looked like a bloodied towel, he recoiled, waving the women on.

Sampson remained until the nuns got to the gate then he returned to his jeep. It didn't take him more than a few minutes to reach the hacienda and just as he pulled up he heard gunfire coming from the street. His heart sank.

He sprinted through the house to the front windows where he could see one nun rushing to get the cart inside the front door, the other was laying on the footpath in front of the house.

"Hurry Mr Peters, the girl is in the laundry bag, you must get her and leave. Now!" Sister Clarita was whispering to him, pointing towards the heavy bag on the cart.

"What happened? What happened to Sister Sofia?" there was no hiding the panic in his voice.

"She is fine, she tripped and fell, I think she has a twisted ankle. I will go and help her now, but you must take the girl and go. Straight away, quickly!"

Sampson was still looking out at the street and realised then that the gunshots had come from the carload of drunk rebels letting off steam outside the cantina. He sprang into action.

Unloading the bag, taking the dazed young woman out, throwing her over his shoulder and running to the jeep. He laid her gently on the back seat, covering her with an old blanket. He stopped for moment then ran back inside.

"Sister, I had a large budget to bring this girl home but with your help it hasn't cost me anywhere near that. I want you to have the rest."

Sister Clarita took the envelope gratefully, standing on tiptoes to kiss Sampson's cheek.

"Thank you, my son. Your work is important, God will keep you safe."

Sampson turned and left. He drove carefully to the outskirts of town then he put his foot down, racing his precious cargo to the airport where a private plane waited to return her to her family.

Three days later as he sat on the hotel balcony waiting for his next assignment, Sampson said a little 'thank you' prayer, the first time he'd spoken to God in many years.

One Tree – One Day

She sits on the white plastic lawn chair from Bunnings, a cup of tea in her hand, looking out at the big old gum tree across the road. In a reminiscing mood, just content to sit and absorb the atmosphere and watch the sky turn pink, then gold, then blue, as the dawn finally arrives.

Her gaze drifts over to the old tree and she notices how impressive it looks, perhaps a little old and tired, but it still stands proudly against the back drop of other trees and bushes and the roof tops of the new housing estate in the distance. Its branches splayed against the cloudless sky, tirelessly supporting twigs, leaves, nuts and even the odd flower.

It occurs to her that she is a lot like that tree, sometimes oblivious to what is going on around her, other times a central part of the surrounding activity. In fact, the tree could be said to be representative of her own journey through life, in many ways. She too has grown from a tiny seed, a long time ago. She has been bent, twisted, shaped by the elements, and her environment, as a child, just like a sapling that sways in the wind.

The old gum is fully grown now and stands majestically tall. She pictures its four main branches signifying her four beautiful children, although one branch appears to have stopped growing upwards and is somewhat shorter than the rest. Her mind wanders to the precious daughter she lost many years ago and a tear springs to her eye, winding its way slowly down her cheek as it usually does when she thinks of her little girl, now in heaven.

The other branches, she sees, grow apart. Spreading in various directions at the top, but are forever joined to the main trunk at the base, and this ultimately provides the magnificent shape of the complete tree.

She notes the most colourful part of the tree – the hundreds of leaves. It reminds her of the people whose lives she has touched, or whose lives have touched hers. She takes a closer look.

There are some new, fresh green ones at the top – the people she has met most recently, there are some bigger, more solidly attached, perfectly formed leaves – the friends and family she has grown so close to over her seventy-four years on this earth. Scattered around the base are some dead leaves that have dropped off the tree over the years for various reasons. Even these are essential to the tree's existence she thinks, providing mulch for the roots during times of drought. She wonders if the tree remembers those leaves as she sits, closes her eyes and ponders the memories of friends passed on.

Peering at the leaves on the tree she is aware that some are turning brown, slowly, like the drifting apart of friends who move on in their lives, taking a different direction to her. There are even a few crinkled and ugly leaves, she chuckles and wonders if the tree would rather be rid of those ones...

Standing close to the gum are two smaller trees. One is a straight, shiny evergreen, with thousands of tiny leaves – and she smiles to herself as she remembers her first husband.

A weedy, tall man who was always popular, but tended to live in a world of his own, not the family man she had once hoped he would be. Sure, he knew lots of people, but they certainly weren't his *friends*.

He really didn't have any big, solid leaves, or indeed any distinct branches, he just stuck straight up out of the ground, all by himself. Still, every tree has a purpose she believed…and it had been fun and a learning adventure – those few years they had together.

To the other side of the gum was an extra-large Tuart tree. Definitely her second husband she muses. Solid and complex and been around forever. The branches all seem to lean towards the gum tree, and smaller branches and leaves appear to be intermingled between the two trees, forever entwined like the love of her life had been with her. He'd made his mark on her heart like the massive branches of the Tuart had on the gum, even stunting its growth in some areas, but helping it to find different directions to grow in others. Closing her eyes, the memories fill her with warmth until a cool breeze wafts over her.

Glancing upwards she notices a flock of birds heading north for the winter, and she thinks about the tree and how, over the years, it must have provided shelter for many creatures. It makes her think of the many different houses she has lived in and how she has turned them into homes for her children. She remembers the hundreds of people who have passed through those homes, friends, kids sleepovers and how her homes, have provided shelter and comfort to family members in times of crisis.

A sudden burst of laughter and the happy chatter of children bring her back from her reverie and she watches as two little boys and their mother stoop to gather gum nuts from the base of the tree. "Look Mummy, here's another perfect one."

"Well you be sure and thank this beautiful old tree," their mother replies, "For providing such lovely gum nuts for our craft day."

The old woman, with a smile on her face, remembers her own children when they were small and how they loved their craft days. All the times she has sat at the kitchen table creating childish masterpieces and home-made Christmas presents. The amount of times she has nurtured her family and sometimes their friends, through sport, games, cooking lessons and how she taught them to tie their shoe-laces and use chop sticks. Her mind wanders to the times she has provided nourishment over the years. The carefully planned healthy meals, the yummy morning and afternoon teas, the celebrations, parties and the quiet hot chocolates shared with a forlorn teenager at midnight. Yes, like the tree she has nurtured, nourished and met the needs of people and animals alike…and she has loved doing so.

As she sits, she comes to realize that the day has passed, so quickly, and she watches as the sun slowly starts to sink, turning the sky a golden colour, then pink and finally dark blue to black. How rapidly our life passes by she thinks. It seems like just a few minutes ago she was watching the dawn break in the east.

She sighs, slowly rising from her chair, and it occurs to her that like the tree, her roots, while still firmly planted in the ground are getting frail and brittle, and how it would only take one big storm or a bulldozer determined to clear a path for a new housing estate for the tree to be gone. Although, with any luck the seasons have been kind and spread the seeds of the old gum far and wide.

For it would be nice, she thinks to herself, if the next generation could sit where she has sat and watch a new young gum break through the soil and slowly become a sapling, to be bent and twisted and shaped by its environment – just like she has been.

Hot Chocolate

She placed the mug on the bench, like she'd done so many times before. The kettle boiled and let loose its high pitch squeal. Almost robotically she put two spoons of chocolate into the mug, adding water, then stirring in a slosh of whiskey, just as he liked it. A smile played across her lips as she added just a dash more.

With a hasty sideways glance towards the front room she drew the vial from her pocket and added the contents to the mix. She'd considered the bitter taste and prepared well by introducing the whiskey months ago. He would never be able to tell now.

Placing the mug on the tray she took it in to her husband of thirty-seven years. She put it on the side table and gathered the empty beer bottles scattered around his chair. Thwack!

His hand came down sharply on her bottom. "Forgot the bloody biscuit again. What the hell is wrong with you? You losing your mind?" he drawled in his alcoholic haze.

She mumbled an apology and hastened back to the kitchen where she fumbled with the biscuit tin. Thump! Crash!

Her heart stopped and she froze to the spot. Don't tell me he discovered it? Perhaps the whiskey hadn't masked the bitterness like she'd planned.

Maria risked a peek around the door frame to the lounge…she turned back. A huge grin travelled across her face. "Free at last," she sighed. She busied herself making another hot chocolate and went to retrieve the other mug before calling the ambulance.

Hostage

Splash! His foot slipped off the curb and into the overflowing drain. "Dammit," he muttered, making his way around to the driver's side door, ripping it open and body slamming into the seat of his yellow cab. He shook his head like a dog, spraying droplets of water all over the dashboard and inside the side window. "Bloody rain."

Hank had just finished his meal break at his favourite Denny's Diner and used the sleeve of his windbreaker to wipe his glasses and dab at the little rivulets of water still trickling down his neck. He turned the car on to start the heat and proceeded to note the time in his work book. "Ok, time to start again," he said to no-one. Turning on his mini computer screen and GPS he rubbed his hands together to warm them and took a quick look up and down the street, although the chances of picking up a street fare in this wild weather were slim. No-one in his right mind would stand out on the street to wave down a cab tonight.

Bringing his gaze back to the inside of the car Hank noticed a scrap of white up in the top left corner of the windscreen. Leaning forward he squinted at the glass and realised it was a folded notepaper, about the size of a small envelope and it was stuck to the outside of his windscreen. "Good Lord!" Hank exclaimed as he proceeded to get out again and make his way around the front of the car to peel the paper off the windscreen. Once he'd returned and gone through the whole drying his face and glasses process again he held the paper in front of the vent.

It had cranked up to full heat and was blowing out hot air so he used it to dry the paper off. It didn't take long. Carefully he opened the folded note and read the cryptic message written in lipstick.

HELP ME APARTMENT 6 HOSTAGE it said.

Hank turned the paper over a few times, looking for any further explanation but there were no other markings. Hmmm, he pondered. What on earth do we have here? He sat, puzzling what he should do next. He shuffled over towards the passenger seat and looked out the window to the street. Slightly behind him was the Denny's Diner, next to that a narrow alleyway, then there was a four storey walk up, followed by a laundromat and a couple of other stores. Looking along this side of the street there didn't appear to be any other residences for at least another block and the other side was taken up with a TJ Maxx next to an empty lot, so no joy there either.

He guessed the writer must mean the walk up. There really wasn't anything else here. He knew the paper wasn't there when he pulled up, so the only way it could have landed there was to float down from one of the windows of the walk up.

Then it would have stuck to the wet windscreen while he was having his meal. It certainly couldn't have been there any longer than that otherwise it would have deteriorated more from the weather.

Hank picked up his cell phone and dialled. "Hi honey, you finished your dinner yet?" the sing song lilt of his wife Anna still seemed like music to his ears, even after fifteen years of wedded bliss.

"Yup. All finished. But a strange thing just happened babe," he replied.

"What? What is it?" she asked, a little curiosity mixed with a hint of worry had crept into her voice. "There's nothing wrong is there? You're ok, aren't you?"

"I'm fine babe. Don't worry. It's just that I got back to the cab and noticed a note on the windscreen. I opened it up and it has a message, written in pink lipstick."

"Oh, that's weird. What does it say?" Anna's voice inquisitive now.

"Well, that's just it. It's kind of strange. Cryptic even. It says HELP ME APARTMENT 6 HOSTAGE."

"Good grief. Did you say HOSTAGE?"

"Yes, HOSTAGE. What do you think it means?" Hank asked her.

"Well I don't know honey, but it certainly sounds mysterious. Maybe even a little creepy. Perhaps you should ring the police, or pop in to the station and drop the note to them? You can't take too much time from your shift though sweetheart. You need to get back on the road. Why don't you wait till your shift is over then head down to the local precinct? I'm sure they will be able to look into it." Anna was always being practical, he loved that about her.

"Yes, you're right of course. I'll drop it off at 11pm when I finish up. Thanks Anna. You get back to your studies darling. I love you. See you a little after 11.30pm then," Hank blew a kiss into the phone.

"Ok Hanky. Drive safe honey. See you later," and she was gone.

Hank turned the paper over in his hands one more time and looked up towards the second floor of the walk up.

There were no lights on at either of the front windows on that floor, but the next floor had what appeared to be lamplight coming from the net curtains at the window on the left. It was then that he noticed that the window was ever so slightly ajar.

Well, that seems funny, on a night like this. Who would leave their windows open with this pouring rain and howling wind? he asked himself. He sat for another couple of minutes, staring up at the window. At one point he imagined that he saw a shadow pass by the window, but it could easily have been his mind playing tricks he thought. Hank made a sudden decision, grabbed his cell phone, a yellow delivery envelope from the glove box and ventured back out into the rain.

Quickly making for the sidewalk and the overhang from the laundromat he took a breath and walked calmly towards the lobby door of the apartment building. Surprisingly the door opened and he hurried inside to shelter from the rain. Usually the buildings in this neighbourhood were secure, so the front door opening was unusual. Hank noticed twelve mail boxes, indicating three apartments on each floor so he knew apartment six would be located on the second floor. Rustling up a bit of courage and standing tall he proceeded up the stairs to the first landing. When he reached the second floor he took in the layout. There appeared to be an apartment at the back, one at the front and one off to the side of the passage.

The numbering must start from the back because he could make out a number six on the door to the front apartment from his vantage point at the top of the stairs. Well, he'd come this far, might as well keep going. When sitting in the safety of his car down on the street it had been easy to think he could just go up and knock on the door and check out the situation. He had planned to say he had a delivery envelope for apartment six, then, if questioned he would realise it was an eight, apologise and be on his way. It had seemed a good plan at the time. However, confronted with the ominous closed door his imagination was now running wild and he didn't feel as confident now. Still, he was doing the right thing so he should just hurry up and get it over with, he admonished himself.

Hank rapped on the door. He was greeted with silence.

He knocked again. This time he thought he heard movement behind the door.

Once again, he knocked, a little louder and more incessantly this time. He called out, "Delivery."

"What is it?" a gruff male voice came back from the still firmly closed front door.

"Delivery sir, yellow cabs," Hank called out, as he often needed to when delivering parcels during his shift.

"Alright, I'm coming," the voice answered and Hank could hear a slide bolt, then a dead bolt being opened. The door swung open and he was surprised to see a rather weedy man sitting in a wheel chair. "Come in, come in," the man said as he turned away and started wheeling towards a coffee table in the centre of a very neat and tidy living room.

"I've got my glasses over here, hang on till I find them and put them on."

Hank hesitated for a moment then stepped into the apartment sensing that he had indeed got this completely wrong as there was obviously nothing going on here in this clean looking, nicely furnished apartment with this disabled young man. He glanced around and took in the slightly masculine décor. "Nice place you have here," he said, making light conversation.

At that moment he heard the door slam behind him. He looked towards it and saw that it was on a spring closer, unusual for a wooden front door as he had only ever seen them used for screen doors. By the time he had turned back to the man in the wheel chair he felt a sting in his arm and could barely comprehend that the man had risen from the chair, taken two large strides and was now standing right next to him!

"Wwwhaaaa…."

Thud.

Hank fell to the floor. He was out cold.

Doug, the man from the wheel chair chuckled. He pressed a button on an intercom on the wall inside the front door and said, "Ok Tom, bring Dave with you, I've got another one for you."

He quickly removed the cell phone, wallet, yellow envelope and folded note from Hank, placed them in a Ziploc bag and waited for the boys to arrive. He took Hank's keys and put them on the bench for later. He'd dispose of the car down at the Brooklyn chop-shop as soon as he could in the morning.

It only took them a couple of minutes to get to the apartment from the basement where they had been playing a game of poker while waiting for Doug's call. "Nice one Dougie, we'll get a pretty penny for him I'll bet. He looks like a good, healthy specimen." The three of them worked like a well-oiled machine to lift Hank on to a sheet of black plastic, gently covering his face with a light material that he could breathe through. They carefully wrapped him tightly, leaving his head out and then placed him on a folding trolley they had brought up for this purpose. They were ready to leave within five minutes.

"See you next Tuesday Dougie for another one," Tom said as he and Dave took their leave. Five minutes later they were loading Hank into the beat-up ambulance parked at the rear of the laundromat. They had done this many times before and wearing their paramedic uniforms had never had any trouble getting in or out of the building. Yes, Tom thought to himself. We'll get at least a thousand for this guy. He drove carefully, to avoid any unnecessary attention, to the clinic in Harlem where the docs would be waiting to harvest the vital, lifesaving organs.

Upstairs Doug was sitting at his desk, sans wheelchair. He was writing a note…it said

HELP ME APARTMENT 6 HOSTAGE

Life is a Garden

Life is a garden, mankind its plants,
Some are big, tall trees, other's flowers, small as ants.

Many have branches, with thousands of leaves,
Few have dead ones, for family they grieve.

The beds are full of colours – beautiful and bold,
Seedlings spring up from roots, gnarled and old.

So, when He rests by the gate, on an old wooden post,
He ponders their fate, and what he likes most.

By far it's the fact that these magnificent creations,
Will keep popping up for many generations.

Forbidden

Sobbing, she turned to Brian. He had always been her rock. Her older, wiser brother, comforting her when she got scared, helping her when she fell off her bike, even picking her up when she called him in the middle of the night, drunk and alone. He never once ratted her out to their mum and dad.

And now they would forever have an even stronger bond. One that would tie them together on another level, forever. A deep, dark secret that only three people knew, or could ever know. Brian, her and Phillip, although of course he wouldn't be telling anyone – because he was now laying there in front of them both – in a casket.

Oh, he does look dapper, she thought. I fell in love with him the first time I saw him in a suit. Her mind wandered back to a time when she had smiled, laughed, and waited eagerly for him to come home from the office. She would be at the door with a cold beer, grab his briefcase and smother him with kisses. More often than not they would end up fooling around on the couch before he'd even got his tie off!

That seemed like a lifetime ago now, although only four years in real time. When had he changed? she wondered. What had been the turning point in their relationship? She wasn't sure she could put a date on it but things certainly got a lot worse when he had started drinking more and that had happened around the time they were told they weren't going to be able to have kids.

Fresh tears streamed down her face as she remembered that horrid, sinking feeling she got as the doctor told them that due to the years of abuse Veronica had suffered as a child at the hands of her father and his brother, Uncle Frank, she had been rendered unable to conceive.

This had been gut wrenchingly hard to come to terms with, Veronica retreating into herself, becoming moody and sullen, Phillip had turned to drinking to cope. At first his drinking had been staying for a few each night after work, but as he got demoted, then finally lost his job, he took to bringing cartons of beer home with him after going to the unemployment office. He would sit on the porch, night after night, morose, not eating his dinner, staying out there alone till the early hours of the morning. When he did sleep he would flop onto the spare bed, the one in what would have become the baby's room. She would hear him sobbing but felt unable to go to him, unable to comfort him, as she herself needed him to comfort her.

It didn't take long for that behaviour to progress to ill temper and raising his voice to her. He even started playing the 'blame game'.

Brian held her a little tighter, feeling her shiver.

"You ok sis? Are you cold? Do you want me to get your jacket from the car?"

He was always so considerate, genuinely caring about her. An older brother yes, but only by two minutes and five seconds. As kids they had enjoyed confusing people at school, their friends and relatives, as their mum had always dressed them similarly, with the same style haircuts.

Veronica had never really thought much about why her Mumma had gone out of her way to dress her like a boy, but last night when Veronica and Brian had been reminiscing she had finally realised that it had been to try to protect her daughter.

Mumma knew what her husband and Uncle Frank had been doing, so she had tried to make Veronica seem more unappealing. She would never have had the courage to do anything about it, to say anything, but she tried, in her own way to deter them.

As they grew up and became teenagers, then young adults Veronica had become much more petite and feminine. Brian however was slightly taller, and had a somewhat 'muscular build' he had become a ruggedly handsome man – she smiled inwardly as she remembered those rippling muscles, the way she had caressed them these past few nights, the way their sweaty bodies had fitted so well together.... she loved that they no longer had to share their special secret with her horrible husband. Now that he was safely disposed of it left her free to spend the rest of her life making herself, and her beautiful brother happy.

Honey, I'm Home

Avoiding the dew covered grass he slipped around the side of the cottage, down the path, through the gate and around the back. He knew his way of course, having replayed this scene in his mind a hundred times. Stealthily he crept up to the sliding door. With a light rattle backwards and forwards he jiggled the door. The catch slid open easily. He closed the door noiselessly behind him.

Dan took a moment to catch his breath then tip-toed across the carpet to the kitchen. He quietly put his work bag on the floor, knowing that he would need that later. He had long ago made the decision to carry one of those canvas duffle bags. Great for hiding all sorts of things, he grinned to himself.

He softly opened drawers until he found a large kitchen knife. "That should do it," he muttered under his breath. Dan slowly proceeded up the passage to the bedroom where he knew she would be sleeping alone. He crept to the door, listening to the soft breathing coming from inside. He loved this bit. That moment before the shock. The seconds of peace and quiet before all hell would break loose.

He grinned, throwing open the door. "Honey, I'm home!" Springing through the door he thrust the bouquet of roses at his new bride. He'd quickly cut the tag off with the knife in the kitchen and now he scooped Hannah up into his arms trying to forget the seven months they had just spent apart while he was at the war front. "I love you sweetheart. Thank God you're home, safe and sound," his loving wife's voice, still soft from sleep was the sweetest sound he had ever heard.

Blood Red

"I don't like red, you know that, I told you..." He mumbled, shaking his head as he scrubbed the stained floor. Even in death it felt as though she was tormenting him. Her gnarled, arthritic fingers reaching from beyond her freshly dug grave; pulling his strings, making him dance to her twisted, self-indulgent tune.

His mind wandered back, back to a time when he was a small boy. He could not remember being happy then, but he vaguely recalled a time when she hadn't treated him badly. When his sister Verity was alive. He smiled to himself as he remembered his sister fondly. She was a beautiful girl, with long braids and porcelain-like skin. Throughout her short, sickly time here on earth he could not remember her grumbling or complaining, not once.

He remembered for a long time after Verity passed, Mother had retreated to her bedroom, hardly speaking to anyone. He was made to take meals to her twice a day and he would often finish his evening chores by cleaning up the beer bottles surrounding Father who was passed out in his chair. He'd turn off the black and white television in the lounge room and take himself off to bed. He spent hours looking out the skylight in the attic roof, above his makeshift cot, dreaming of travelling to the stars and planets.

Finished scrubbing now he rinsed out the bucket, threw the bloody rags into the furnace and soaked the mop head with bleach. Returning to Mother's bedroom he nodded, pleased with his excellent clean-up job.

All those years of looking after his parents had finally paid off. Keeping house for them for over twenty five of his thirty-two years. He sighed, thinking as he often did, Father had got out of things rather easily by dying of liver cancer all those years ago.

As he moved around the room, unconsciously tidying, straightening the bedcovers, picking up clothes and folding them neatly, his eyes were drawn to the door in the far wall. His heart skipped a beat as he realized he would no longer have to go into that room. He would not have to endure that daily ritual, those atrocities. He was finding it hard to fully comprehend what that meant for him now and just how much his life would change. He lingered over the chair where she used to sit with him when he was small, where she would put him over her knee and...

Stop! He admonished himself. *You do not have to re-live this. It's over, finally it's over. Don't let her continue to control you.* Frustrated with himself he strode over to the antique dressing table which was as neat as a pin. In the centre, taking pride of place - her hair brush. How many times had he endured that brush?

His eyes rested on the big tub of powder with its fluffy pink powder puff on top and he felt guilty as he remembered how it used to tickle. His glance took in all the lipsticks standing like toy soldiers in a row.

He picked up a vial of lavender water, nearly empty. She would use it on him several times a day, to 'mask his horrid male animal scent' she would tell him. He dropped it into the waste basket next to the dressing table.

He lifted the hair net and turned it over gently in his hands. She had used it to keep his perfectly braided hair in place overnight. He smirked as that too made its way into the basket.

He was filled now with a new emotion. Anger. Boiling and bubbling under his skin for so long. Now he could let it out. He let out a wolf-like howl and swept his arm across the dressing table, all the tubs, vials, bottles and tubes spilling over the side. *There* he thought, *that's better. All cleaned up.* He went to turn away and noticed one lonely lipstick remaining on the outer edge of the dressing table. He snatched it up and was about to send it flying into the basket with its companions when he noticed the shade written on the bottom of the tube. Slowly he begun to laugh. The chortling gained momentum. It built like a crescendo at the end of an opera. He fell to the bed, laughing maniacally, tears streaming from his eyes. This was the one he hated being made to wear the most, and he'd never even known its name. Through his laughter he mumbled, over and over ... "Illicit Lovers - Blood Red."

Jude St Clair

The author lives in Mandurah, Western Australia. She has a Bachelor of Commerce, majoring in Marketing and Management, which she obtained as a mature age student while raising her family of four children. She loves to read and write and has been an enthusiastic participant in amateur theatre for over 20 years.

Jude won the Society of Women Writers September Writers' Marathon in both 2015 and 2016 and has attained second and third place in two other marathons. This is the first of two books of short stories she has published.

She believes in promoting reading and writing for children and adults alike at a local level and is a member of two local writers' groups, where she contributes weekly. She is also a member of Sisters in Crime, a group based in Melbourne that provides support for women mystery writers.

Jude loves to travel and experience new things. She wouldn't consider herself an adrenalin junky but she does like to enjoy life to the fullest. She has parachuted, white water rafted, ridden a mechanical bull, parasailed, hitch hiked around Australia, ridden a Harley, currently drives a convertible and has twice lived in New Orleans.